PR
4070
.E96
v.5

Barrie, Sir James Matthew, bart., 1860-1937.
    The novels, tales and sketches of J. M.
Barrie. New York, C. Scribner's sons,
1896-1911.
    12 v. fronts. (v. 1 : port.) plates.
22 cm.
On verse of t.p. : Author's edition.
    CONTENTS.--v. 1. Auld licht idylls.
Better dead.--v. 2. When a man's single.--
v. 3. A window in Thrums. An Edinburgh
eleven.--v. 4-5. The little minister.--

(continued next card)

J. M. BARRIE

VOL. V

THE LITTLE MINISTER

AIRLIE CASTLE

From a photograph.

AIRLIE CASTLE.
From a photograph.

THE NOVELS, TALES AND SKETCHES OF J. M. BARRIE 🐦 🐦 🐦

THE LITTLE MINISTER

PART II

🐦 PUBLISHED IN NEW YORK BY CHARLES SCRIBNER'S SONS 🐦 🐦 1896 🐦

AUTHOR'S EDITION

J. M. Barrie

CONTENTS

PART II

PAGE

XX END OF THE STATE OF INDECISION . 241

XXI NIGHT — MARGARET — FLASHING OF A LANTERN 254

XXII LOVERS. 267

XXIII CONTAINS A BIRTH, WHICH IS SUF-FICIENT FOR ONE CHAPTER . . 279

XXIV THE NEW WORLD, AND THE WO-MAN WHO MAY NOT DWELL THEREIN 287

XXV BEGINNING OF THE TWENTY-FOUR HOURS 295

XXVI SCENE AT THE SPITTAL 306

XXVII FIRST JOURNEY OF THE DOMINIE TO THRUMS DURING THE TWENTY-FOUR HOURS 316

XXVIII THE HILL BEFORE DARKNESS FELL —SCENE OF THE IMPENDING CATASTROPHE 323

XXIX STORY OF THE EGYPTIAN 333

XXX THE MEETING FOR RAIN 344

XXXI VARIOUS BODIES CONVERGING ON THE HILL 354

XXXII LEADING SWIFTLY TO THE APPALL-ING MARRIAGE 366

XXXIII WHILE THE TEN O'CLOCK BELL WAS RINGING 374

XXXIV THE GREAT RAIN 383

XXXV THE GLEN AT BREAK OF DAY . . 388

v

CONTENTS

                                                              PAGE

XXXVI   STORY OF THE DOMINIE 407

XXXVII SECOND JOURNEY OF THE DOMI-
        NIE TO THRUMS DURING THE
        TWENTY-FOUR HOURS 420

XXXVIII THRUMS DURING THE TWENTY-
        FOUR HOURS — DEFENCE OF
        THE MANSE 430

XXXIX   HOW BABBIE SPENT THE NIGHT
        OF AUGUST FOURTH 442

XL   BABBIE AND MARGARET — DEFENCE
        OF THE MANSE (CONTINUED) . . 450

XLI   RINTOUL AND BABBIE—BREAK-
        DOWN OF THE DEFENCE OF
        THE MANSE 460

XLII   MARGARET, THE PRECENTOR, AND
        GOD BETWEEN 470

XLIII   RAIN—MIST—THE JAWS 481

XLIV   END OF THE TWENTY-FOUR
        HOURS 494

XLV   TALK OF A LITTLE MAID SINCE
        GROWN TALL 502

THE LITTLE MINISTER

PART II

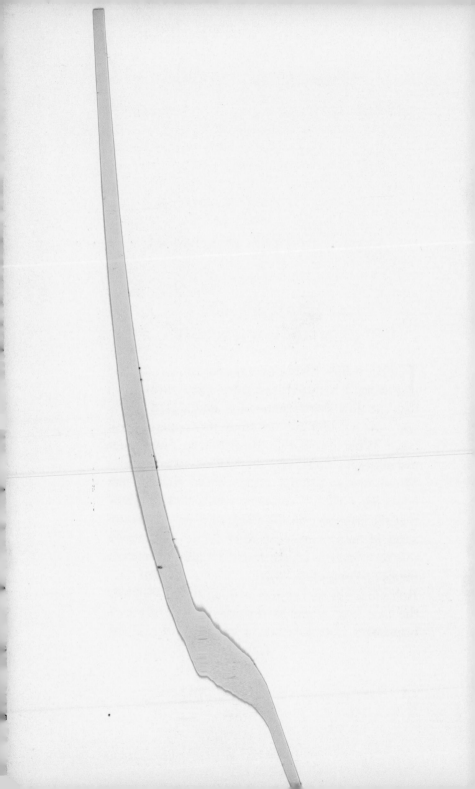

THE LITTLE MINISTER

CHAPTER XX

END OF THE STATE OF INDECISION

LONG before I had any thought of writing this story, I had told it so often to my little maid that she now knows some of it better than I. If you saw me looking up from my paper to ask her, " What was it that Birse said to Jean about the minister's flowers? " or, " Where was Hendry Munn hidden on the night of the riots? " and heard her confident answers, you would conclude that she had been in the thick of these events, instead of born many years after them. I mention this now because I have reached a point where her memory contradicts mine. She maintains that Rob Dow was told of the meeting in the wood by the two boys whom it disturbed, while my own impression is that he was a witness of it. If she

is right, Rob must have succeeded in frightening
the boys into telling no other person, for certainly
the scandal did not spread in Thrums.   After all,
however, it is only important to know that Rob
did learn of the meeting.   Its first effect was to
send him sullenly to the drink.

Many a time since these events have I pictured
what might have been their upshot had Dow con-
fided their discovery to me.   Had I suspected
why Rob was grown so dour again, Gavin's future
might have been very different.   I was meeting
Rob now and again in the glen, asking, with an
affected carelessness he did not bottom, for news
of the little minister, but what he told me was
only the gossip of the town; and what I should
have known, that Thrums might never know it,
he kept to himself.   I suppose he feared to speak
to Gavin, who made several efforts to reclaim him,
but without avail.

Yet Rob's heart opened for a moment to one
man, or rather was forced open by that man.   A
few days after the meeting at the well, Rob was
bringing the smell of whisky with him down
Banker's Close when he ran against a famous staff,
with which the doctor pinned him to the wall.

" Ay," said the outspoken doctor, looking con-
temptuously into Rob's bleary eyes, "so this is
what your conversion amounts to?   Faugh!   Rob
Dow, if you were half a man the very thought of

what Mr. Dishart has done for you would make you run past the public-houses."

"It's the thocht o' him that sends me running to them," growled Rob, knocking down the staff. "Let me alane."

"What do you mean by that?" demanded McQueen, hooking him this time.

"Speir at himsel'; speir at the woman."

"What woman?"

"Take your staff out o' my neck."

"Not till you tell me why you, of all people, are speaking against the minister."

Torn by a desire for a confidant and loyalty to Gavin, Rob was already in a fury.

"Say again," he burst forth, "that I was speaking agin the minister and I'll practise on you what I'm awid to do to her."

"Who is she?"

"Wha's wha?"

"The woman whom the minister ——"

"I said nothing about a woman," said poor Rob, alarmed for Gavin. "Doctor, I'm ready to swear afore a bailie that I never saw them thegither at the Kaims."

"The Kaims!" exclaimed the doctor, suddenly enlightened. "Pooh! you only mean the Egyptian. Rob, make your mind easy about this. I know why he met her there."

"Do you ken that she has bewitched him; do

you ken I saw him trying to put his arms round her; do you ken they have a trysting-place in Caddam wood?"

This came from Rob in a rush, and he would fain have called it all back.

"I'm drunk, doctor, roaring drunk," he said, hastily, "and it wasna the minister I saw ava; it was another man."

Nothing more could the doctor draw from Rob, but he had heard sufficient to smoke some pipes on. Like many who pride themselves on being recluses, McQueen loved the gossip that came to him uninvited; indeed, he opened his mouth to it as greedily as any man in Thrums. He respected Gavin, however, too much to find this new dish palatable, and so his researches to discover whether other Auld Lichts shared Rob's fears were conducted with caution. "Is there no word of your minister's getting a wife yet?" he asked several, but only got for answers, "There's word o' a Glasgow leddy's sending him baskets o' flowers," or "He has his een open, but he's taking his time; ay, he's looking for the blade o' corn in the stack o' chaff."

This convinced McQueen that the congregation knew nothing of the Egyptian, but it did not satisfy him, and he made an opportunity of inviting Gavin into the surgery. It was, to the doctor, the cosiest nook in his house, but to me and many others a room that smelled of hearses. On the top of the pipes and tobacco tins that littered the table there usually lay a death certificate, placed there deliberately by the doctor to scare his sister, who had a passion for putting the surgery to rights.

"By the way," McQueen said, after he and Gavin had talked a little while, "did I ever advise you to smoke?"

"It is your usual form of salutation," Gavin answered, laughing. "But I don't think you ever supplied me with a reason."

"I daresay not. I am too experienced a doctor to cheapen my prescriptions in that way. However, here is one good reason. I have noticed, sir, that at your age a man is either a slave to a pipe or to a woman. Do you want me to lend you a pipe now?"

"Then I am to understand," asked Gavin, slyly, "that your locket came into your possession in your pre-smoking days, and that you merely wear it from habit?"

"Tuts!" answered the doctor, buttoning his coat. "I told you there was nothing in the locket. If there is, I have forgotten what it is."

"You are a hopeless old bachelor, I see," said Gavin, unaware that the doctor was probing him. He was surprised next moment to find McQueen in the ecstasies of one who has won a rubber.

"Now, then," cried the jubilant doctor, "as you

have confessed so much, tell me all about her. Name and address, please."

"Confess! What have I confessed?"

"It won't do, Mr. Dishart, for even your face betrays you. No, no, I am an old bird, but I have not forgotten the ways of the fledglings. 'Hopeless bachelor,' sir, is a sweetmeat in every young man's mouth until of a sudden he finds it sour, and that means the banns. When is it to be?"

"We must find the lady first," said the minister, uncomfortably.

"You tell me, in spite of that face, that you have not fixed on her?"

"The difficulty, I suppose, would be to persuade her to fix on me."

"Not a bit of it. But you admit there is some one?"

"Who would have me?"

"You are wriggling out of it. Is it the banker's daughter?"

"No," Gavin cried.

"I hear you have walked up the back wynd with her three times this week. The town is in a ferment about it."

"She is a great deal in the back wynd."

"Fiddle-de-dee! I am oftener in the back wynd than you, and I never meet her there."

"That is curious."

"No, it isn't, but never mind. Perhaps you

246

have fallen to Miss Pennycuick's piano? Did you hear it going as we passed the house?"

"She seems always to be playing on her piano."

"Not she; but you are supposed to be musical, and so when she sees you from her window she begins to thump. If I am in the school wynd and hear the piano going, I know you will turn the corner immediately. However, I am glad to hear it is not Miss Pennycuick. Then it is the factor at the Spittal's lassie? Well done, sir. You should arrange to have the wedding at the same time as the old earl's, which comes off in summer, I believe."

"One foolish marriage is enough in a day, doctor."

"Eh? You call him a fool for marrying a young wife? Well, no doubt he is, but he would have been a bigger fool to marry an old one. However, it is not Lord Rintoul we are discussing, but Gavin Dishart. I suppose you know that the factor's lassie is an heiress?"

"And, therefore, would scorn me."

"Try her," said the doctor, drily. "Her father and mother, as I know, married on a ten-pound note. But if I am wrong again, I must adopt the popular view in Thrums. It is a Glasgow lady after all? Man, you needn't look indignant at hearing that the people are discussing your intended. You can no more stop it than a doctor's orders could keep Lang Tammas out of church.

They have discovered that she sends you flowers twice every week."

" They never reach me," answered Gavin, then remembered the holly and winced.

"Some," persisted the relentless doctor, "even speak of your having been seen together; but of course, if she is a Glasgow lady, that is a mistake."

" Where did they see us?" asked Gavin, with a sudden trouble in his throat.

" You are shaking," said the doctor, keenly, " like a medical student at his first operation. But as for the story that you and the lady have been seen together, I can guess how it arose. Do you remember that gypsy girl?"

The doctor had begun by addressing the fire, but he suddenly wheeled round and fired his question in the minister's face. Gavin, however, did not even blink.

"Why should I have forgotten her?" he replied, coolly.

" Oh, in the stress of other occupations. But it was your getting the money from her at the Kaims for Nanny that I was to speak of. Absurd though it seems, I think some dotard must have seen you and her at the Kaims, and mistaken her for the lady."

McQueen flung himself back in his chair to enjoy this joke.

"Fancy mistaking that woman for a lady!" he said to Gavin, who had not laughed with him.

" I think Nanny has some justification for considering her a lady," the minister said, firmly.

" Well, I grant that. But what made me guffaw was a vision of the harum-scarum, devil-may-care little Egyptian mistress of an Auld Licht manse!"

" She is neither harum-scarum, nor devil-may-care," Gavin answered without heat, for he was no longer a distracted minister. " You don't understand her as I do."

" No, I seem to understand her differently."

" What do you know of her?"

" That is just it," said the doctor, irritated by Gavin's coolness. " I know she saved Nanny from the poorhouse, but I don't know where she got the money. I know she can talk fine English when she chooses, but I don't know where she learned it. I know she heard that the soldiers were coming to Thrums before they knew of their destination themselves, but I don't know who told her. You who understand her can doubtless explain these matters?"

" She offered to explain them to me," Gavin answered, still unmoved, " but I forbade her."

" Why?"

" It is no business of yours, doctor. Forgive me for saying so."

" In Thrums," replied McQueen, " a minister's business is everybody's business. I have often wondered who helped her to escape from the soldiers that night. Did she offer to explain that to you?"

"She did not."

"Perhaps," said the doctor, sharply, "because it was unnecessary?"

"That was the reason."

"You helped her to escape?"

"I did."

"And you are not ashamed of it?"

"I am not."

"Why were you so anxious to screen her?"

"She saved some of my people from gaol."

"Which was more than they deserved."

"I have always understood that you concealed two of them in your own stable."

"Maybe I did," the doctor had to allow. "But I took my stick to them next morning. Besides, they were Thrums folk, while you had never set eyes on that imp of mischief before."

"I cannot sit here, doctor, and hear her called names," Gavin said, rising, but McQueen gripped him by the shoulder.

"For pity's sake, sir, don't let us wrangle like a pair of women. I brought you here to speak my mind to you, and speak it I will. I warn you, Mr. Dishart, that you are being watched. You have been seen meeting this lassie in Caddam as well as at the Kaims."

"Let the whole town watch, doctor. I have met her openly."

"And why? Oh, don't make Nanny your excuse."

"I won't. I met her because I love her."

"Are you mad?" cried McQueen. "You speak as if you would marry her."

"Yes," replied Gavin, determinedly, "and I mean to do it."

The doctor flung up his hands.

"I give you up," he said, raging. "I give you up. Think of your congregation, man."

"I have been thinking of them, and as soon as I have a right to do so I shall tell them what I have told you."

"And until you tell them I will keep your madness to myself, for I warn you that, as soon as they do know, there will be a vacancy in the Auld Licht kirk of Thrums."

"She is a woman," said Gavin, hesitating, though preparing to go, "of whom any minister might be proud."

"She is a woman," the doctor roared, "that no congregation would stand. Oh, if you will go, there is your hat."

Perhaps Gavin's face was whiter as he left the house than when he entered it, but there was no other change. Those who were watching him decided that he was looking much as usual, except

251

that his mouth was shut very firm, from which they concluded that he had been taking the doctor to task for smoking. They also noted that he returned to McQueen's house within half an hour after leaving it, but remained no time.

Some explained this second visit by saying that the minister had forgotten his cravat, and had gone back for it. What really sent him back, however, was his conscience. He had said to McQueen that he helped Babbie to escape from the soldiers because of her kindness to his people, and he returned to own that it was a lie.

Gavin knocked at the door of the surgery, but entered without waiting for a response. McQueen was no longer stamping through the room, red and furious. He had even laid aside his pipe. He was sitting back in his chair, looking half-mournfully, half-contemptuously, at something in his palm. His hand closed instinctively when he heard the door open, but Gavin had seen that the object was an open locket.

"It was only your reference to the thing," the detected doctor said, with a grim laugh, "that made me open it. Forty years ago, sir, I —— Phew! it is forty-two years, and I have not got over it yet." He closed the locket with a snap. "I hope you have come back, Dishart, to speak more rationally?"

END OF THE STATE OF INDECISION

Gavin told him why he had come back, and the doctor said he was a fool for his pains.

" Is it useless, Dishart, to make another appeal to you ? "

" Quite useless, doctor," Gavin answered, promptly. " My mind is made up at last."

CHAPTER XXI

THAT evening the little minister sat silently in his parlour. Darkness came, and with it weavers rose heavy-eyed from their looms, sleepy children sought their mothers, and the gate of the field above the manse fell forward to let cows pass to their byre; the great Bible was produced in many homes, and the ten o'clock bell clanged its last word to the night. Margaret had allowed the lamp to burn low. Thinking that her boy slept, she moved softly to his side and spread her shawl over his knees. He had forgotten her. The doctor's warnings scarcely troubled him. He was Babbie's lover. The mystery of her was only a veil hiding her from other men, and he was looking through it upon the face of his beloved.

It was a night of long ago, but can you not see my dear Margaret still as she bends over her son? Not twice in many days dared the minister snatch a moment's sleep from grey morning to midnight, and, when this did happen, he jumped up by-and-by in shame, to revile himself for an idler and ask his mother wrathfully why she had not tumbled

254

him out of his chair? To-night Margaret was divided between a desire to let him sleep and a fear of his self-reproach when he awoke; and so, perhaps, the tear fell that roused him.

"I did not like to waken you," Margaret said, apprehensively. "You must have been very tired, Gavin?"

"I was not sleeping, mother," he said, slowly. "I was only thinking."

"Ah, Gavin, you never rise from your loom. It is hardly fair that your hands should be so full of other people's troubles."

"They only fill one hand, mother; I carry the people's joys in the other hand, and that keeps me erect, like a woman between her pan and pitcher. I think the joys have outweighed the sorrows since we came here."

"It has been all joy to me, Gavin, for you never tell me of the sorrows. An old woman has no right to be so happy."

"Old woman, mother!" said Gavin. But his indignation was vain. Margaret was an old woman. I made her old before her time.

"As for these terrible troubles," he went on, "I forget them the moment I enter the garden and see you at your window. And, maybe, I keep some of the joys from you as well as the troubles."

Words about Babbie leaped to his mouth, but with an effort he restrained them. He must not

tell his mother of her until Babbie of her free will
had told him all there was to tell.

"I have been a selfish woman, Gavin."

"You selfish, mother!" Gavin said, smiling.
"Tell me when you did not think of others before
yourself?"

"Always, Gavin. Has it not been selfishness
to hope that you would never want to bring another
mistress to the manse? Do you remember how
angry you used to be in Glasgow when I said
that you would marry some day?"

"I remember," Gavin said, sadly.

"Yes; you used to say, 'Don't speak of such
a thing, mother, for the horrid thought of it is
enough to drive all the Hebrew out of my head.'
Was not that lightning just now?"

"I did not see it. What a memory you have,
mother, for all the boyish things I said."

"I can't deny," Margaret admitted with a sigh,
"that I liked to hear you speak in that way,
though I knew you would go back on your word.
You see, you have changed already."

"How, mother?" asked Gavin, surprised.

"You said just now that those were boyish
speeches. Gavin, I can't understand the mothers
who are glad to see their sons married; though I
had a dozen I believe it would be a wrench to
lose one of them. It would be different with
daughters. You are laughing, Gavin!"

"Yes, at your reference to daughters. Would you not have preferred me to be a girl?"

"'Deed I would not," answered Margaret, with tremendous conviction. "Gavin, every woman on earth, be she rich or poor, good or bad, offers up one prayer about her firstborn, and that is, 'May he be a boy!'"

"I think you are wrong, mother. The banker's wife told me that there is nothing for which she thanks the Lord so much as that all her children are girls."

"May she be forgiven for that, Gavin!" exclaimed Margaret; "though she maybe did right to put the best face on her humiliation. No, no, there are many kinds of women in the world, but there never was one yet that didn't want to begin with a laddie. You can speculate about a boy so much more than about a girl. Gavin, what is it a woman thinks about the day her son is born? yes, and the day before too? She is picturing him a grown man, and a slip of a lassie taking him from her. Ay, that is where the lassies have their revenge on the mothers. I remember as if it were this morning a Harvie fishwife patting your head and asking who was your sweetheart, and I could never thole the woman again. We were at the door of the cottage, and I mind I gripped you up in my arms. You had on a tartan frock with a sash and diamond socks. When I look back, Gavin, it seems to me that you have shot up from that frock to manhood in a single hour."

"There are not many mothers like you," Gavin said, laying his hand fondly on Margaret's shoulder.

"There are many better mothers, but few such sons. It is easily seen why God could not afford me another. Gavin, I am sure that was lightning."

"I think it was; but don't be alarmed, mother."

"I am never frightened when you are with me."

"And I always will be with you."

"Ah, if you were married ——"

"Do you think," asked Gavin, indignantly, "that it would make any difference to you?"

Margaret did not answer. She knew what a difference it would make.

"Except," continued Gavin, with a man's obtuseness, "that you would have a daughter as well as a son to love you and take care of you."

Margaret could have told him that men give themselves away needlessly who marry for the sake of their mother, but all she said was —

"Gavin, I see you can speak more composedly of marrying now than you spoke a year ago. If I did not know better, I should think a Thrums young lady had got hold of you."

It was a moment before Gavin replied; then he said, gaily —

"Really, mother, the way the best of women speak of each other is lamentable. You say I should be better married, and then you take for granted that every marriageable woman in the neighbourhood is trying to kidnap me. I am sure you did not take my father by force in that way."

He did not see that Margaret trembled at the mention of his father. He never knew that she was many times pining to lay her head upon his breast and tell him of me. Yet I cannot but believe that she always shook when Adam Dishart was spoken of between them. I cannot think that the long-cherishing of the secret which was hers and mine kept her face steady when that horror suddenly confronted her as now. Gavin would have suspected much had he ever suspected anything.

"I know," Margaret said, courageously, "that you would be better married; but when it comes to selecting the woman I grow fearful. Oh, Gavin!" she said, earnestly, "it is an awful thing to marry the wrong man!"

Here in a moment had she revealed much, though far from all, and there must have been many such moments between them. But Gavin was thinking of his own affairs.

"You mean the wrong woman, don't you, mother?" he said, and she hastened to agree. But it was the wrong man she meant.

"The difficulty, I suppose, is to hit upon the right one?" Gavin said, blithely.

" To know which is the right one in time," answered Margaret, solemnly. "But I am saying nothing against the young ladies of Thrums, Gavin. Though I have scarcely seen them, I know there are good women among them. Jean says —— "

" I believe, mother," Gavin interposed, reproachfully, " that you have been questioning Jean about them ? "

" Just because I was afraid — I mean because I fancied — you might be taking a liking to one of them."

" And what is Jean's verdict ? "

" She says every one of them would jump at you, like a bird at a berry."

" But the berry cannot be divided. How would Miss Pennycuick please you, mother ? "

" Gavin ! " cried Margaret, in consternation, " you don't mean to —— But you are laughing at me again."

" Then there is the banker's daughter ? "

" I can't thole her."

" Why, I question if you ever set eyes on her, mother."

" Perhaps not, Gavin ; but I have suspected her ever since she offered to become one of your tract distributors."

" The doctor," said Gavin, not ill-pleased, " was saying that either of these ladies would suit me.'

"What business has he," asked Margaret, vindictively, "to put such thoughts into your head?"

"But he only did as you are doing. Mother, I see you will never be satisfied without selecting the woman for me yourself."

"Ay, Gavin," said Margaret, earnestly; "and I question if I should be satisfied even then. But I am sure I should be a better guide to you than Dr. McQueen is."

"I am convined of that. But I wonder what sort of woman would content you?"

"Whoever pleased you, Gavin, would content me," Margaret ventured to maintain. "You would only take to a clever woman."

"She must be nearly as clever as you, mother."

"Hoots, Gavin," said Margaret, smiling, "I'm not to be caught with chaff. I am a stupid, ignorant woman."

"Then I must look out for a stupid, ignorant woman, for that seems to be the kind I like," answered Gavin, of whom I may confess here something that has to be told sooner or later. It is this: he never realised that Babbie was a great deal cleverer than himself. Forgive him, you who read, if you have any tolerance for the creature, man.

"She will be terribly learned in languages," pursued Margaret, "so that she may follow you in your studies, as I have never been able to do."

"Your face has helped me more than Hebrew, mother," replied Gavin. "I will give her no marks for languages."

"At any rate," Margaret insisted, "she must be a grand housekeeper, and very thrifty."

"As for that," Gavin said, faltering a little, "one can't expect it of a mere girl."

"I should expect it," maintained his mother.

"No, no; but she would have you," said Gavin, happily, "to teach her housekeeping."

"It would be a pleasant occupation to me, that," Margaret admitted. "And she would soon learn; she would be so proud of her position as mistress of a manse."

"Perhaps," Gavin said, doubtfully. He had no doubt on the subject in his college days.

"And we can take for granted," continued his mother, "that she is a lassie of fine character."

"Of course," said Gavin, holding his head high, as if he thought the doctor might be watching him.

"I have thought," Margaret went on, "that there was a great deal of wisdom in what you said at that last marriage in the manse, the one where, you remember, the best man and the bridesmaid joined hands instead of the bride and bridegroom."

"What did I say?" asked the little minister, with misgivings.

"That there was great danger when people married out of their own rank of life."

" Oh — ah — well, of course, that would depend on circumstances."

" They were wise words, Gavin. There was the sermon, too, that you preached a month or two ago against marrying into other denominations. Jean told me that it greatly impressed the congregation. It is a sad sight, as you said, to see an Auld Licht lassie changing her faith because her man belongs to the U. P.'s."

" Did I say that ? "

" You did, and it so struck Jean that she told me she would rather be an old maid for life, ' the which,' she said, ' is a dismal prospect,' than marry out of the Auld Licht kirk."

" Perhaps that was a rather narrow view I took, mother. After all, the fitting thing is that the wife should go with her husband; especially if it is he that is the Auld Licht."

" I don't hold with narrowness myself, Gavin," Margaret said, with an effort, " and I admit that there are many respectable persons in the other denominations. But though a weaver might take a wife from another kirk without much scandal, an Auld Licht minister's madam must be Auld Licht born and bred. The congregation would expect no less. I doubt if they would be sure of her if she came from some other Auld Licht kirk. 'Deed, though she came from our own kirk I'm thinking the session would want to catechise her. Ay, and if all you tell me of Lang Tammas be true (for, as you know, I never spoke to him), I warrant he would catechise the session."

"I would brook no interference from my session," said Gavin, knitting his brows, "and I do not consider it necessary that a minister's wife should have been brought up in his denomination. Of course she would join it. We must make allowance, mother, for the thousands of young women who live in places where there is no Auld Licht kirk."

"You can pity them, Gavin," said Margaret, "without marrying them. A minister has his congregation to think of."

"So the doctor says," interposed her son.

"Then it was just like his presumption!" cried Margaret. "A minister should marry to please himself."

"Decidedly he should," Gavin agreed, eagerly, "and the bounden duty of the congregation is to respect and honour his choice. If they forget that duty, his is to remind them of it."

"Ah, well, Gavin," said Margaret, confidently, "your congregation are so fond of you that your choice would doubtless be theirs. Jean tells me that even Lang Tammas, though he is so obstinate, has a love for you passing the love of woman. These were her words. Jean is more sentimental than you might think."

"I wish he would show his love," said Gavin, "by contradicting me less frequently."

"You have Rob Dow to weigh against him."

"No; I cannot make out what has come over Rob lately. He is drinking heavily again, and avoiding me. The lightning is becoming very vivid."

"Yes, and I hear no thunder. There is another thing, Gavin. I am one of those that like to sit at home, but if you had a wife she would visit the congregation. A truly religious wife would be a great help to you."

"Religious," Gavin repeated slowly. "Yes, but some people are religious without speaking of it. If a woman is good she is religious. A good woman who has been, let us say, foolishly brought up, only needs to be shown the right way to tread it. Mother, I question if any man, minister or layman, ever yet fell in love because the woman was thrifty, or clever, or went to church twice on Sabbath."

"I believe that is true," Margaret said, "and I would not have it otherwise. But it is an awful thing, Gavin, as you said from the pulpit two weeks ago, to worship only at a beautiful face."

"You think too much about what I say in the pulpit, mother," Gavin said, with a sigh, "though of course a man who fell in love merely with a face would be a contemptible creature. Yet I see that women do not understand how beauty affects a man."

"Yes, yes, my boy—oh, indeed, they do," said Margaret, who on some matters knew far more than her son.

Twelve o'clock struck, and she rose to go to bed, alarmed lest she should not waken early in the morning. "But I am afraid I shan't sleep," she said, "if that lightning continues."

"It is harmless," Gavin answered, going to the window. He started back next moment, and crying, "Don't look out, mother," hastily pulled down the blind.

"Why, Gavin," Margaret said in fear, "you look as if it had struck you."

"Oh, no," Gavin answered, with a forced laugh, and he lit her lamp for her.

But it had struck him, though it was not lightning. It was the flashing of a lantern against the window to attract his attention, and the holder of the lantern was Babbie.

"Good-night, mother."

"Good-night, Gavin. Don't sit up any later."

CHAPTER XXII

LOVERS

ONLY something terrible, Gavin thought, could have brought Babbie to him at such an hour; yet when he left his mother's room it was to stand motionless on the stair, waiting for a silence in the manse that would not come. A house is never still in darkness to those who listen intently; there is a whispering in distant chambers, an unearthly hand presses the snib of the window, the latch rises. Ghosts were created when the first man woke in the night.

Now Margaret slept. Two hours earlier, Jean, sitting on the salt-bucket, had read the chapter with which she always sent herself to bed. In honour of the little minister she had begun her Bible afresh when he came to Thrums, and was progressing through it, a chapter a night, sighing, perhaps, on washing days at a long chapter, such as Exodus twelfth, but never making two of it. The kitchen wag-at-the-wall clock was telling every room in the house that she had neglected to shut her door. As Gavin felt his way down

267

the dark stair, awakening it into protest at every step, he had a glimpse of the pendulum's shadow running back and forward on the hearth; he started back from another shadow on the lobby wall, and then seeing it start too, knew it for his own. He opened the door and passed out unobserved; it was as if the sounds and shadows that filled the manse were too occupied with their game to mind an interloper.

"Is that you?" he said to a bush, for the garden was in semi-darkness. Then the lantern's flash met him, and he saw the Egyptian in the summer-seat.

"At last!" she said, reproachfully. "Evidently a lantern is a poor door-bell."

"What is it?" Gavin asked, in suppressed excitement, for the least he expected to hear was that she was again being pursued for her share in the riot. The tremor in his voice surprised her into silence, and he thought she faltered because what she had to tell him was so woeful. So, in the darkness of the summer-seat, he kissed her, and she might have known that with that kiss the little minister was hers for ever.

Now Babbie had been kissed before, but never thus, and she turned from Gavin, and would have liked to be alone, for she had begun to know what love was, and the flash that revealed it to her laid bare her own shame, so that her impulse was to hide herself from her lover. But of all this Gavin was unconscious, and he repeated his question. The lantern was swaying in her hand, and when she turned fearfully to him its light fell on his face, and she saw how alarmed he was.

"I am going away back to Nanny's," she said suddenly, and rose cowed, but he took her hand and held her.

"Babbie," he said, huskily, "tell me what has happened to bring you here at this hour."

She sought to pull her hand from him, but could not.

"How you are trembling!" he whispered. "Babbie," he cried, "something terrible has happened to you, but do not fear. Tell me what it is, and then — then I will take you to my mother: yes, I will take you now."

The Egyptian would have given all she had in the world to be able to fly from him then, that he might never know her as she was, but it could not be, and so she spoke out remorselessly. If her voice had become hard, it was a new-born scorn of herself that made it so.

"You are needlessly alarmed," she said; "I am not at all the kind of person who deserves sympathy or expects it. There is nothing wrong. I am staying with Nanny over-night, and only came to Thrums to amuse myself. I chased your policeman down the Roods with my lantern, and then came here to amuse myself with you. That is all."

"It was nothing but a love of mischief that brought you here?" Gavin asked, sternly, after an unpleasant pause.

"Nothing," the Egyptian answered, recklessly.

"I could not have believed this of you," the minister said; "I am ashamed of you."

"I thought," Babbie retorted, trying to speak lightly until she could get away from him, "that you would be glad to see me. Your last words in Caddam seemed to justify that idea."

"I am very sorry to see you," he answered, reproachfully.

"Then I will go away at once," she said, stepping out of the summer-seat.

"Yes," he replied, "you must go at once."

"Then I won't," she said, turning back defiantly. "I know what you are to say: that the Thrums people would be shocked if they knew I was here; as if I cared what the Thrums people think of me."

"I care what they think of you," Gavin said, as if that were decisive, "and I tell you I will not allow you to repeat this freak."

"You 'will not allow me,'" echoed Babbie, almost enjoying herself, despite her sudden loss of self-respect.

"I will not," Gavin said resolutely. "Henceforth you must do as I think fit."

"Since when have you taken command of me?" demanded Babbie.

"Since a minute ago," Gavin replied, "when you let me kiss you."

"Let you!" exclaimed Babbie, now justly incensed. "You did it yourself. I was very angry."

"No, you were not."

"I am not allowed to say that even?" asked the Egyptian. "Tell me something I may say, then, and I will repeat it after you."

"I have something to say to you," Gavin told her, after a moment's reflection; "yes, and there is something I should like to hear you repeat after me, but not to-night."

"I don't want to hear what it is," Babbie said, quickly, but she knew what it was, and even then, despite the new pain at her heart, her bosom swelled with pride because this man still loved her. Now she wanted to run away with his love for her before he could take it from her, and then realising that this parting must be for ever, a great desire filled her to hear him put that kiss into words, and she said, faltering:

"You can tell me what it is if you like."

"Not to-night," said Gavin.

"To-night, if at all," the gypsy almost entreated.

"To-morrow, at Nanny's," answered Gavin, decisively: and this time he remembered without dismay that to-morrow was the Sabbath.

In the fairy tale the beast suddenly drops his skin and is a prince, and I believe it seemed to Babbie that some such change had come over this man, her plaything.

"Your lantern is shining on my mother's window," were the words that woke her from this discovery, and then she found herself yielding the lantern to him. She became conscious vaguely that a corresponding change was taking place in herself.

"You spoke of taking me to your mother," she said, bitterly.

"Yes," he answered at once, "to-morrow;" but she shook her head, knowing that to-morrow he would be wiser.

"Give me the lantern," she said, in a low voice, "I am going back to Nanny's now."

"Yes," he said, "we must set out now, but I can carry the lantern."

"You are not coming with me!" she exclaimed, shaking herself free of his hand.

"I am coming," he replied, calmly, though he was not calm. "Take my arm, Babbie."

She made a last effort to free herself from bondage, crying passionately, "I will not let you come."

"When I say I am coming," Gavin answered between his teeth, "I mean that I am coming, and so let that be an end of this folly. Take my arm."

LOVERS

" I think I hate you," she said, retreating from him.

" Take my arm," he repeated, and, though her breast was rising rebelliously, she did as he ordered, and so he escorted her from the garden. At the foot of the field she stopped, and thought to frighten him by saying, " What would the people say if they saw you with me now ? "

" It does not much matter what they would say," he answered, still keeping his teeth together as if doubtful of their courage. " As for what they would do, that is certain; they would put me out of my church."

" And it is dear to you ? "

" Dearer than life."

" You told me long ago that your mother's heart would break if——"

" Yes, I am sure it would."

They had begun to climb the fields, but she stopped him with a jerk.

" Go back, Mr. Dishart," she implored, clutching his arm with both hands. " You make me very unhappy for no purpose. Oh, why should you risk so much for me ? "

" I cannot have you wandering here alone at midnight," Gavin answered, gently.

" That is nothing to me," she said, eagerly, but no longer resenting his air of proprietorship.

" You will never do it again if I can prevent it."

273

"But you cannot," she said, sadly. "Oh, yes, you can, Mr. Dishart. If you will turn back now I shall promise never to do anything again without first asking myself whether it would seem right to you. I know I acted very wrongly tonight."

"Only thoughtlessly," he said.

"Then have pity on me," she besought him, "and go back. If I have only been thoughtless, how can you punish me thus? Mr. Dishart," she entreated, her voice breaking, "if you were to suffer for this folly of mine, do you think I could live?"

"We are in God's hands, dear," he answered, firmly, and he again drew her arm to him. So they climbed the first field, and were almost at the hill before either spoke again.

"Stop," Babbie whispered, crouching as she spoke; "I see some one crossing the hill."

"I have seen him for some time," Gavin answered, quietly; "but I am doing no wrong, and I will not hide."

The Egyptian had to walk on with him, and I suppose she did not think the less of him for that. Yet she said, warningly —

"If he sees you, all Thrums will be in an uproar before morning."

"I cannot help that," Gavin replied. "It is the will of God."

"To ruin you for my sins?"

"If He thinks fit."

The figure drew nearer, and with every step Babbie's distress doubled.

"We are walking straight to him," she whispered. "I implore you to wait here until he passes, if not for your own sake, for your mother's."

At that he wavered, and she heard his teeth sliding against each other, as if he could no longer clench them.

"But, no," he said, moving on again, "I will not be a skulker from any man. If it be God's wish that I should suffer for this, I must suffer."

"Oh, why," cried Babbie, beating her hands together in grief, "should you suffer for me?"

"You are mine," Gavin answered. Babbie gasped. "And if you act foolishly," he continued, "it is right that I should bear the brunt of it. No, I will not let you go on alone; you are not fit to be alone. You need some one to watch over you and care for you and love you, and, if need be, to suffer with you."

"Turn back, dear, before he sees us."

"He has seen us."

Yes, I had seen them, for the figure on the hill was no other than the dominie of Glen Quharity. The park gate clicked as it swung to, and I looked up and saw Gavin and the Egyptian. My eyes should have found them sooner, but it was to gaze

275

upon Margaret's home, while no one saw me, that I had trudged into Thrums so late, and by that time, I suppose, my eyes were of little service for seeing through. Yet, when I knew that of these two people suddenly beside me on the hill one was the little minister and the other a strange woman, I fell back from their side with dread before I could step forward and cry "Gavin!"

"I am Mr. Dishart," he answered, with a composure that would not have served him for another sentence. He was more excited than I, for the "Gavin" fell harmlessly on him, while I had no sooner uttered it than there rushed through me the shame of being false to Margaret. It was the only time in my life that I forgot her in him, though he has ever stood next to her in my regard.

I looked from Gavin to the gypsy woman, and again from her to him, and she began to tell a lie in his interest. But she got no farther than "I met Mr. Dishart accid——" when she stopped, ashamed. It was reverence for Gavin that checked the lie. Not every man has had such a compliment paid him.

"It is natural," Gavin said, slowly, "that you, sir, should wonder why I am here with this woman at such an hour, and you may know me so little as to think ill of me for it."

I did not answer, and he misunderstood my silence.

" No," he continued, in a harder voice, as if I
had asked him a question, " I will explain nothing
to you. You are not my judge. If you would
do me harm, sir, you have it in your power."

It was with these cruel words that Gavin addressed me. He did not know how cruel they
were. The Egyptian, I think, must have seen
that his suspicions hurt me, for she said, softly,
with a look of appeal in her eyes —

" You are the schoolmaster in Glen Quharity? Then you will perhaps save Mr. Dishart the
trouble of coming farther by showing me the way
to old Nanny Webster's house at Windyghoul?"

" I have to pass the house at any rate," I answered eagerly, and she came quickly to my side.

I knew, though in the darkness I could see but
vaguely, that Gavin was holding his head high
and waiting for me to say my worst. I had not
told him that I dared think no evil of him, and
he still suspected me. Now I would not trust
myself to speak lest I should betray Margaret, and
yet I wanted him to know that base doubts about
him could never find a shelter in me. I am a
timid man who long ago lost the glory of my life
by it, and I was again timid when I sought to let
Gavin see that my faith in him was unshaken. I
lifted my bonnet to the gypsy, and asked her to
take my arm. It was done clumsily, I cannot
doubt, but he read my meaning and held out his

277

hand to me. I had not touched it since he was three years old, and I trembled too much to give it the grasp I owed it. He and I parted without a word, but to the Egyptian he said, "To-morrow, dear, I will see you at Nanny's," and he was to kiss her, but I pulled her a step farther from him, and she put her hands over her face, crying, "No, no!"

If I asked her some questions between the hill and Windyghoul you must not blame me, for this was my affair as well as theirs. She did not answer me; I know now that she did not hear me. But at the mud house she looked abruptly into my face, and said —

"You love him, too!"

I trudged to the school-house with these words for company, and it was less her discovery than her confession that tortured me. How much I slept that night you may guess.

CHAPTER XXIII

CONTAINS A BIRTH, WHICH IS SUFFICIENT FOR ONE CHAPTER

"The kirk bell will soon be ringing," Nanny said on the following morning, as she placed herself carefully on a stool, one hand holding her Bible and the other wandering complacently over her aged merino gown. "Ay, lassie, though you're only an Egyptian I would hae ta'en you wi' me to hear Mr. Duthie, but it's speiring ower muckle o' a woman to expect her to gang to the kirk in her ilka day claethes."

The Babbie of yesterday would have laughed at this, but the new Babbie sighed.

"I wonder you don't go to Mr. Dishart's church now, Nanny," she said, gently. "I am sure you prefer him."

"Babbie, Babbie," exclaimed Nanny, with spirit, "may I never be so far left to mysel' as to change my kirk just because I like another minister better! It's easy seen, lassie, that you ken little o' religious questions."

"Very little," Babbie admitted, sadly.

"But dinna be so waeful about it," the old wo-

279

man continued, kindly, "for that's no nane like you. Ay, and if you see muckle mair o' Mr. Dishart he'll soon cure your ignorance."

"I shall not see much more of him," Babbie answered, with averted head.

"The like o' you couldna expect it," Nanny said, simply, whereupon Babbie went to the window. "I had better be stepping," Nanny said, rising, "for I am aye late unless I'm on the hill by the time the bell begins. Ay, Babbie, I'm doubting my merino's no sair in the fashion?"

She looked down at her dress half despondently, and yet with some pride.

"It was fowerpence the yard, and no less," she went on, fondling the worn merino, "when we bocht it at Sam'l Curr's. Ay, but it has been turned sax times since syne."

She sighed, and Babbie came to her and put her arms round her, saying, "Nanny, you are a dear."

"I'm a gey auld-farrant-looking dear, I doubt," said Nanny, ruefully.

"Now, Nanny," rejoined Babbie, "you are just wanting me to flatter you. You know the merino looks very nice."

"It's a guid merino yet," admitted the old woman, "but, oh, Babbie, what does the material matter if the cut isna fashionable? It's fine, isn't it, to be in the fashion?"

She spoke so wistfully that, instead of smiling, Babbie kissed her.

"I am afraid to lay hand on the merino, Nanny, but give me off your bonnet and I'll make it ten years younger in as many minutes."

"Could you?" asked Nanny, eagerly, unloosening her bonnet-strings. "Mercy on me!" she had to add; "to think about altering bonnets on the Sabbath-day! Lassie, how could you propose sic a thing?"

"Forgive me, Nanny," Babbie replied, so meekly that the old woman looked at her curiously.

"I dinna understand what has come ower you," she said. "There's an unca difference in you since last nicht. I used to think you were mair like a bird than a lassie, but you've lost a' your daft capers o' singing and lauching, and I take ill wi't. Twa or three times I've catched you greeting. Babbie, what has come ower you?"

"Nothing, Nanny. I think I hear the bell."

Down in Thrums two kirk-officers had let their bells loose, waking echoes in Windyghoul as one dog in country parts sets all the others barking, but Nanny did not hurry off to church. Such a surprising notion had filled her head suddenly that she even forgot to hold her dress off the floor.

"Babbie," she cried, in consternation, "dinna tell me you've gotten ower fond o' Mr. Dishart."

"The like of me, Nanny!" the gypsy answered,

with affected raillery, but there was a tear in her eye.

" It would be a wild, presumptious thing," Nanny said, "and him a grand minister, but——"

Babbie tried to look her in the face, but failed, and then all at once there came back to Nanny the days when she and her lover wandered the hill together.

"Ah, my dawtie," she cried, so tenderly, "what does it matter wha he is when you canna help it!"

Two frail arms went round the Egyptian, and Babbie rested her head on the old woman's breast. But do you think it could have happened had not Nanny loved a weaver two-score years before?

And now Nanny has set off for church and Babbie is alone in the mud house. Some will pity her not at all, this girl who was a dozen women in the hour, and all made of impulses that would scarce stand still to be photographed. To attempt to picture her at any time until now would have been like chasing a spirit that changes to something else as your arms clasp it; yet she has always seemed a pathetic little figure to me. If I understand Babbie at all, it is, I think, because I loved Margaret, the only woman I have ever known well, and one whose nature was not, like the Egyptian's, complex, but most simple, as if God had told her only to be good. Throughout my life since she came into it she has been to me a glass in which many things are revealed that I could not have learned save through her, and something of all womankind, even of bewildering Babbie, I seem to know because I knew Margaret.

No woman is so bad but we may rejoice when her heart thrills to love, for then God has her by the hand. There is no love but this. She may dream of what love is, but it is only of a sudden that she knows. Babbie, who was without a guide from her baby days, had dreamed but little of it, hearing its name given to another thing. She had been born wild and known no home; no one had touched her heart except to strike it; she had been educated, but never tamed; her life had been thrown strangely among those who were great in the world's possessions, but she was not of them. Her soul was in such darkness that she had never seen it; she would have danced away cynically from the belief that there is such a thing, and now all at once she had passed from disbelief to knowledge. Is not love God's doing? To Gavin He had given something of Himself, and the moment she saw it the flash lit her own soul.

It was but little of his Master that was in Gavin, but far smaller things have changed the current of human lives; the spider's thread that strikes our brow on a country road may do that. Yet this I will say, though I have no wish to cast the little minister on my pages larger than he was, that he had some heroic hours in Thrums, of which one was when Babbie learned to love him. Until the moment when he kissed her she had only conceived him a quaint fellow whose life was a string of Sundays, but behold what she saw in him now. Evidently to his noble mind her mystery was only some misfortune, not of her making, and his was to be the part of leading her away from it into the happiness of the open life. He did not doubt her, for he loved, and to doubt is to dip love in the mire. She had been given to him by God, and he was so rich in her possession that the responsibility attached to the gift was not grievous. She was his, and no mortal man could part them. Those who looked askance at her were looking askance at him; in so far as she was wayward and wild, he was those things; so long as she remained strange to religion, the blame lay on him.

All this Babbie read in the Gavin of the past night, and to her it was the book of love. What things she had known, said and done in that holy name! How shamefully have we all besmirched it! She had only known it as the most selfish of the passions, a brittle image that men consulted because it could only answer in the words they gave it to say. But here was a man to whom love was something better than his own desires leering on a pedestal. Such love as Babbie had seen hitherto made strong men weak, but this was

CONTAINS A BIRTH

a love that made a weak man strong. All her
life, strength had been her idol, and the weakness
that bent to her cajolery her scorn. But only now
was it revealed to her that strength, instead of being the lusty child of passions, grows by grappling
with and throwing them.

So Babbie loved the little minister for the best
that she had ever seen in man. I shall be told
that she thought far more of him than he deserved,
forgetting the mean in the worthy: but who that
has had a glimpse of heaven will care to let his
mind dwell henceforth on earth? Love, it is said,
is blind, but love is not blind. It is an extra eye,
which shows us what is most worthy of regard.
To see the best is to see most clearly, and it is the
lover's privilege.

Down in the Auld Licht kirk that forenoon
Gavin preached a sermon in praise of Woman,
and up in the mud house in Windyghoul Babbie
sat alone. But it was the Sabbath day to her:
the first Sabbath in her life. Her discovery had
frozen her mind for a time, so that she could only
stare at it with eyes that would not shut; but that
had been in the night. Already her love seemed
a thing of years, for it was as old as herself, as old
as the new Babbie. It was such a dear delight
that she clasped it to her, and exulted over it
because it was hers, and then she cried over it
because she must give it up.

285

For Babbie must only look at this love and then turn from it. My heart aches for the little Egyptian, but the Promised Land would have remained invisible to her had she not realised that it was only for others. That was the condition of her seeing.

CHAPTER XXIV

THE NEW WORLD, AND THE WOMAN WHO MAY NOT DWELL THEREIN

Up here in the glen school-house after my pupils have straggled home, there comes to me at times, and so sudden that it may be while I am infusing my tea, a hot desire to write great books. Perhaps an hour afterwards I rise, beaten, from my desk, flinging all I have written into the fire (yet rescuing some of it on second thoughts), and curse myself as an ingle-nook man, for I see that one can only paint what he himself has felt, and in my passion I wish to have all the vices, even to being an impious man, that I may describe them better. For this may I be pardoned. It comes to nothing in the end, save that my tea is brackish.

Yet though my solitary life in the glen is cheating me of many experiences, more helpful to a writer than to a Christian, it has not been so tame but that I can understand why Babbie cried when she went into Nanny's garden and saw the new world. Let no one who loves be called altogether unhappy. Even love unreturned has its rainbow, and Babbie knew that Gavin loved her. Yet she

287

stood in woe among the stiff berry bushes, as one who stretches forth her hands to Love and sees him looking for her, and knows she must shrink from the arms she would lie in, and only call to him in a voice he cannot hear. This is not a love that is always bitter. It grows sweet with age. But could that dry the tears of the little Egyptian, who had only been a woman for a day?

Much was still dark to her. Of one obstacle that must keep her and Gavin ever apart she knew, and he did not, but had it been removed she would have given herself to him humbly, not in her own longing, but because he wanted her. "Behold what I am," she could have said to him then, and left the rest to him, believing that her unworthiness would not drag him down, it would lose itself so readily in his strength. That Thrums could rise against such a man if he defied it, she did not believe; but she was to learn the truth presently from a child.

To most of us, I suppose, has come some shock that was to make us different men from that hour, and yet, how many days elapsed before something of the man we had been leapt up in us? Babbie thought she had buried her old impulsiveness, and then remembering that from the top of the field she might see Gavin returning from church, she hastened to the hill to look upon him from a distance. Before she reached the gate where I had met her and him, however, she stopped, distressed at her selfishness, and asked bitterly, " Why am I so different from other women; why should what is so easy to them be so hard to me ? "

" Gavin, my beloved ! " the Egyptian cried in her agony, and the wind caught her words and flung them in the air, making sport of her.

She wandered westward over the bleak hill, and by-and-by came to a great slab called the Standing Stone, on which children often sit and muse until they see gay ladies riding by on palfreys — a kind of horse — and knights in glittering armour, and goblins, and fiery dragons, and other wonders now extinct, of which bare-legged laddies dream, as well as boys in socks. The Standing Stone is in the dyke that separates the hill from a fir wood, and it is the fairy-book of Thrums. If you would be a knight yourself, you must sit on it and whisper to it your desire.

Babbie came to the Standing Stone, and there was a little boy astride it. His hair stood up through holes in his bonnet, and he was very ragged and miserable.

" Why are you crying, little boy ? " Babbie asked him, gently; but he did not look up, and the tongue was strange to him.

" How are you greeting so sair ? " she asked.

" I'm no greeting very sair," he answered, turning his head from her that a woman might not see his tears. "I am no greeting so sair but what I grat sairer when my mither died."

"When did she die?" Babbie inquired.

"Lang syne," he answered, still with averted face.

"What is your name?"

"Micah is my name. Rob Dow's my father."

"And have you no brothers nor sisters?" asked Babbie, with a fellow-feeling for him.

"No, juist my father," he said.

"You should be the better laddie to him then. Did your mither no tell you to be that afore she died?"

"Ay," he answered, "she telled me ay to hide the bottle frae him when I could get haud o't. She took me into the bed to make me promise that, and syne she died."

"Does your father drink?"

"He hauds mair than ony other man in Thrums," Micah replied, almost proudly.

"And he strikes you?" Babbie asked, compassionately.

"That's a lie," retorted the boy, fiercely. "Leastwise, he doesna strike me except when he's mortal, and syne I can jouk him."

"What are you doing there?"

"I'm wishing. It's a wishing stane."

"You are wishing your father wouldna drink."

"No, I'm no," answered Micah. "There was

a lang time he didna drink, but the woman has sent him to it again. It's about her I'm wishing. I'm wishing she was in hell."

"What woman is it?" asked Babbie, shuddering.

"I dinna ken," Micah said, "but she's an ill ane."

"Did you never see her at your father's house?"

"Na; if he could get grip o' her he would break her ower his knee. I hearken to him saying that, when he's wild. He says she should be burned for a witch."

"But if he hates her," asked Babbie, "how can she have sic power ower him?"

"It's no him that she has haud o'," replied Micah, still looking away from her.

"Wha is it then?"

"It's Mr. Dishart."

Babbie was struck as if by an arrow from the wood. It was so unexpected that she gave a cry, and then for the first time Micah looked at her.

"How should that send your father to the drink?" she asked, with an effort.

"Because my father's michty fond o' him," answered Micah, staring strangely at her; "and when the folk ken about the woman, they'll stane the minister out o' Thrums."

The wood faded for a moment from the Egyptian's sight. When it came back, the boy had slid off the Standing Stone and was stealing away.

"Why do you run frae me?" Babbie asked, pathetically.

"I'm fleid at you," he gasped, coming to a standstill at a safe distance: "you're the woman!"

Babbie cowered before her little judge, and he drew nearer her slowly.

"What makes you think that?" she said.

It was a curious time for Babbie's beauty to be paid its most princely compliment.

"Because you're so bonny," Micah whispered across the dyke. Her tears gave him courage. "You micht gang awa," he entreated. "If you kent what a differ Mr. Dishart made in my father till you came, you would maybe gang awa. When he's roaring fou I have to sleep in the wood, and it's awfu' cauld. I'm doubting he'll kill me, woman, if you dinna gang awa."

Poor Babbie put her hand to her heart, but the innocent lad continued mercilessly—

"If ony shame comes to the minister, his auld mither'll die. How have you sic an ill will at the minister?"

Babbie held up her hands like a supplicant.

"I'll gie you my rabbit," Micah said, "if you'll gang awa. I've juist the ane." She shook her head, and, misunderstanding her, he cried, with his knuckles in his eye, "I'll gie you them baith, though I'm michty sweer to part wi' Spotty."

Then at last Babbie found her voice.

"Keep your rabbits, laddie," she said, "and greet no more. I'm gaen awa."

"And you'll never come back no more a' your life?" pleaded Micah.

"Never no more a' my life," repeated Babbie.

"And ye'll leave the minister alane for ever and ever?"

"For ever and ever."

Micah rubbed his face dry, and said, "Will you let me stand on the Standing Stane and watch you gaen awa for ever and ever?"

At that a sob broke from Babbie's heart, and looking at her doubtfully Micah said—

"Maybe you're gey ill for what you've done?"

"Ay," Babbie answered, "I'm gey ill for what I've done."

A minute passed, and in her anguish she did not know that still she was standing at the dyke. Micah's voice roused her:

"You said you would gang awa, and you're no gaen."

Then Babbie went away. The boy watched her across the hill. He climbed the Standing Stone and gazed after her until she was but a coloured ribbon among the broom. When she disappeared into Windyghoul he ran home joyfully, and told his father what a good day's work he had done. Rob struck him for a fool for taking a gypsy's word, and warned him against speaking of the woman in Thrums.

But though Dow believed that Gavin continued to meet the Egyptian secretly, he was wrong. A sum of money for Nanny was sent to the minister, but he could guess only from whom it came. In vain did he search for Babbie. Some months passed and he gave up the search, persuaded that he should see her no more. He went about his duties with a drawn face that made many folk uneasy when it was stern, and pained them when it tried to smile. But to Margaret, though the effort was terrible, he was as he had ever been, and so no thought of a woman crossed her loving breast.

CHAPTER XXV

I can tell still how the whole of the glen was engaged about the hour of noon on the fourth of August month; a day to be among the last forgotten by any of us, though it began as quietly as a roaring March. At the Spittal, between which and Thrums this is a halfway house, were gathered two hundred men in kilts, and many gentry from the neighbouring glens, to celebrate the earl's marriage, which was to take place on the morrow, and thither, too, had gone many of my pupils to gather gossip, at which girls of six are trustier hands than boys of twelve. Those of us, however, who were neither children nor of gentle blood, remained at home, the farmers more taken up with the want of rain, now become a calamity, than with an old man's wedding, and their women-folk wringing their hands for rain also, yet finding time to marvel at the marriage's taking place at the Spittal instead of in England, of which the ignorant spoke vaguely as an estate of the bride's.

295

For my own part I could talk of the disastrous
drouth with Waster Lunny as I walked over his
parched fields, but I had not such cause as he to
brood upon it by day and night; and the ins and
outs of the earl's marriage were for discussing at a
tea-table, where there were women to help one to
conclusions, rather than for the reflections of a
solitary dominie, who had seen neither bride nor
bridegroom. So it must be confessed that when
I might have been regarding the sky moodily, or
at the Spittal, where a free table that day invited
all, I was sitting in the school-house, heeling my
left boot, on which I have always been a little
hard.

I made small speed, not through lack of craft,
but because one can no more drive in tackets
properly than take cities unless he gives his whole
mind to it; and half of mine was at the Auld
Licht manse. Since our meeting six months earlier on the hill I had not seen Gavin, but I had
heard much of him, and of a kind to trouble me.

"I saw nothing queer about Mr. Dishart," was
Waster Lunny's frequent story, "till I hearkened
to Elspeth speaking about it to the lasses (for I'm
the last Elspeth would tell onything to, though I'm
her man), and syne I minded I had been noticing
it for months. Elspeth says," he would go on,
for he could no more forbear quoting his wife
than complaining of her, "that the minister'll

listen to you nowadays wi' his een glaring at you as if he had a perfectly passionate interest in what you were telling him (though it may be only about a hen wi' the croup), and then, after all, he hasna heard a sylib. Ay, I listened to Elspeth saying that, when she thoct I was at the byre, and yet, would you believe it, when I says to her after lousing time, ' I've been noticing of late that the minister loses what a body tells him,' all she answers is, ' Havers.' Tod, but women's provoking."

" I allow," Birse said, " that on the first Sabbath o' June month, and again on the third Sabbath, he poured out the Word grandly, but I've ta'en note this curran Sabbaths that if he's no mighty magnificent he's mighty poor. There's something damming up his mind, and when he gets by it he's a roaring water, but when he doesna he's a despisable trickle. The folk thinks it's a woman that's getting in his way, but dinna tell me that about sic a scholar; I tell you he would gang ower a toon o' women like a loaded cart ower new-laid stanes."

Wearyworld hobbled after me up the Roods one day, pelting me with remarks, though I was doing my best to get away from him. " Even Rob Dow sees there's something come ower the minister," he bawled, " for Rob's fou ilka Sabbath now. Ay, but this I will say for Mr. Dishart, that he aye gies me a civil word." I thought I had left the policeman behind with this, but next minute he roared, "and whatever is the matter wi' him it has made him kindlier to me than ever." He must have taken the short cut through Lunan's close, for at the top of the Roods his voice again made up on me. "Dagone you, for a cruel pack to put your fingers to your lugs ilka time I open my mouth."

As for Waster Lunny's daughter Easie, who got her schooling free for redding up the school-house and breaking my furniture, she would never have been off the gossip about the minister, for she was her mother in miniature, with a tongue that ran like a pump after the pans are full, not for use but for the mere pleasure of spilling.

On that awful fourth of August I not only had all this confused talk in my head but reason for jumping my mind between it and the Egyptian (as if to catch them together unawares), and I was like one who, with the mechanism of a watch jumbled in his hand, could set it going if he had the art.

Of the gypsy I knew nothing save what I had seen that night, yet what more was there to learn? I was aware that she loved Gavin and that he loved her. A moment had shown it to me. Now with the Auld Lichts, I have the smith's acquaintance with his irons, and so I could not believe that they would suffer their minister to marry a vagrant. Had it not been for this knowledge, which made me fearful for Margaret, I would have done no-

thing to keep these two young people apart. Some
to whom I have said this maintain that the Egyptian turned my head at our first meeting. Such
an argument is not perhaps worth controverting.
I admit that even now I straighten under the fire
of a bright eye, as a pensioner may salute when he
sees a young officer. In the shooting season,
should I chance to be leaning over my dyke while
English sportsmen pass (as is usually the case if I
have seen them approaching), I remember nought
of them save that they call me "she," and end
their greetings with "whatever" (which Waster
Lunny takes to be a southron mode of speech),
but their ladies dwell pleasantly in my memory,
from their engaging faces to the pretty crumpled
thing dangling on their arms, that is a hat or a
basket, I am seldom sure which. The Egyptian's
beauty, therefore, was a gladsome sight to me, and
none the less so that I had come upon it as unex-
pectedly as some men step into a bog. Had she
been alone when I met her I cannot deny that I
would have been content to look on her face,
without caring what was inside it; but she was
with her lover, and that lover was Gavin, and so
her face was to me as little for admiring as this
glen in a thunderstorm, when I know that some
fellow-creature is lost on the hills.

If, however, it was no quick liking for the gypsy
that almost tempted me to leave these two lovers

to each other, what was it? It was the warning of my own life. Adam Dishart had torn my arm from Margaret's, and I had not recovered the wrench in eighteen years. Rather than act his part between these two I felt tempted to tell them, "Deplorable as the result may be, if you who are a minister marry this vagabond, it will be still more deplorable if you do not."

But there was Margaret to consider, and at thought of her I cursed the Egyptian aloud. What could I do to keep Gavin and the woman apart? I could tell him the secret of his mother's life. Would that be sufficient? It would if he loved Margaret, as I did not doubt. Pity for her would make him undergo any torture rather than she should suffer again. But to divulge our old connection would entail her discovery of me, and I questioned if even the saving of Gavin could destroy the bitterness of that.

I might appeal to the Egyptian. I might tell her even what I shuddered to tell him. She cared for him, I was sure, well enough to have the courage to give him up. But where was I to find her?

Were she and Gavin meeting still? Perhaps the change which had come over the little minister meant that they had parted. Yet what I had heard him say to her on the hill warned me not to trust in any such solution of the trouble.

Boys play at casting a humming-top into the

midst of others on the ground, and if well aimed
it scatters them prettily. I seemed to be playing
such a game with my thoughts, for each new one
sent the others here and there, and so what could
I do in the end but fling my tops aside, and return
to the heeling of my boot?

I was thus engaged when the sudden waking
of the glen into life took me to my window.
There is seldom silence up here, for if the wind be
not sweeping the heather, the Quharity, that I may
not have heard for days, seems to have crept nearer
to the school-house in the night, and if both wind
and water be out of earshot, there is the crack of
a gun, or Waster Lunny's shepherd is on a stone
near at hand whistling, or a lamb is scrambling
through a fence, and kicking foolishly with its
hind legs. These sounds I am unaware of until
they stop, when I look up. Such a stillness was
broken now by music.

From my window I saw a string of people
walking rapidly down the glen, and Waster Lunny
crossing his potato-field to meet them. Remembering that, though I was in my stocking soles,
the ground was dry, I hastened to join the farmer,
for I like to miss nothing. I saw a curious sight.
In front of the little procession coming down the
glen road, and so much more impressive than his
satellites that they may be put out of mind as
merely ploughmen and the like following a show,

was a Highlander that I knew to be Lauchlan Campbell, one of the pipers engaged to lend music to the earl's marriage. He had the name of a thrawn man when sober, but pretty at the pipes at both times, and he came marching down the glen blowing gloriously, as if he had the clan of Campbell at his heels. I know no man who is so capable on occasion of looking like twenty as a Highland piper, and never have I seen a face in such a blaze of passion as was Lauchlan Campbell's that day. His following were keeping out of his reach, jumping back every time he turned round to shake his fist in the direction of the Spittal. While this magnificent man was yet some yards from us, I saw Waster Lunny, who had been in the middle of the road to ask questions, fall back in fear, and not being a fighting man myself, I jumped the dyke. Lauchlan gave me a look that sent me farther into the field, and strutted past, shrieking defiance through his pipes, until I lost him and his followers in a bend of the road.

"That's a terrifying spectacle," I heard Waster Lunny say when the music had become but a distant squeal. "You're bonny at louping dykes, dominie, when there is a wild bull in front o' you. Na, I canna tell what has happened, but at the least Lauchlan maun hae dirked the earl. Thae loons cried out to me as they gaed by that he has been blowing awa' at that tune till he canna halt.

What a wind's in the crittur! I'm thinking there's a hell in ilka Highlandman."

" Take care then, Waster Lunny, that you dinna licht it," said an angry voice that made us jump, though it was only Duncan, the farmer's shepherd, who spoke.

" I had forgotten you was a Highlandman yoursel', Duncan," Waster Lunny said nervously, but Elspeth, who had come to us unnoticed, ordered the shepherd to return to the hillside, which he did haughtily.

"How did you no lay haud on that blast o' wind, Lauchlan Campbell," asked Elspeth of her husband, "and speir at him what had happened at the Spittal? A quarrel afore a marriage brings ill luck."

" I'm thinking," said the farmer, " that Rintoul's making his ain ill luck by marrying on a young leddy."

"A man's never ower auld to marry," said Elspeth.

"No, nor a woman," rejoined Waster Lunny, " when she gets the chance. But, Elspeth, I believe I can guess what has fired that fearsome piper. Depend upon it, somebody has been speaking disrespectful about the crittur's ancestors."

" His ancestors!" exclaimed Elspeth, scornfully. " I'm thinking mine could hae bocht them at a crown the dozen."

303

" Hoots," said the farmer, "you're o' a weaving stock, and dinna understand about ancestors. Take a stick to a Highland laddie, and it's no him you hurt, but his ancestors. Likewise it's his ancestors that stanes you for it. When Duncan stalked awa the now, what think you he saw? He saw a farmer's wife dauring to order about his ancestors; and if that's the way wi' a shepherd, what will it be wi' a piper that has the kilts on him a' day to mind him o' his ancestors ilka time he looks down? "

Elspeth retired to discuss the probable disturbance at the Spittal with her family, giving Waster Lunny the opportunity of saying to me impressively—

" Man, man, has it never crossed you that it's a queer thing the like o' you and me having no ancestors? Ay, we had them in a manner o' speaking, no doubt, but they're as completely lost sicht o' as a flagon lid that's fallen ahint the dresser. Hech, sirs, but they would need a gey rubbing to get the rust off them now. I've been thinking that if I was to get my laddies to say their grandfather's name a curran times ilka day, like the Catechism, and they were to do the same wi' their bairns, and it was continued in future generations, we micht raise a fell field o' ancestors in time. Ay, but Elspeth wouldna hear o't. Nothing angers her mair than to hear me speak o' planting trees for the benefit o' them that's to be farmers here after me, and as for ancestors, she would howk them up as quick as I could plant them. Losh, dominie, is that a boot in your hand ? "

To my mortification I saw that I had run out of the school-house with the boot on my hand as if it were a glove, and back I went straightway, blaming myself for a man wanting in dignity. It was but a minor trouble this, however, even at the time; and to recall it later in the day was to look back on happiness, for though I did not know it yet, Lauchlan's playing raised the curtain on the great act of Gavin's life, and the twenty-four hours had begun, to which all I have told as yet is no more than the prologue.

CHAPTER XXVI

SCENE AT THE SPITTAL

WITHIN an hour after I had left him Waster Lunny walked into the school-house and handed me his snuff-mull, which I declined politely. It was with this ceremony that we usually opened our conversations.

"I've seen the post," he said, "and he tells me there has been a queer ploy at the Spittal. It's a wonder the marriage hasna been turned into a burial, and all because o' that Highland stirk, Lauchlan Campbell."

Waster Lunny was a man who had to retrace his steps in telling a story if he tried short cuts, and so my custom was to wait patiently while he delved through the ploughed fields that always lay between him and his destination.

"As you ken, Rintoul's so little o' a Scotchman that he's no muckle better than an Englisher. That maun be the reason he hadna mair sense than to tramp on a Highlandman's ancestors, as he tried to tramp on Lauchlan's this day."

"If Lord Rintoul insulted the piper," I suggested, giving the farmer a helping hand cautiously, "it would be through inadvertence. Rintoul only bought the Spittal a year ago, and until then, I daresay, he had seldom been on our side of the Border."

This was a foolish interruption, for it set Waster Lunny off in a new direction.

"That's what Elspeth says. Says she, ' When the earl has grand estates in England, what for does he come to a barren place like the Spittal to be married ? It's gey like,' she says, ' as if he wanted the marriage to be got by quietly; a thing,' says she, ' that no woman can stand. Furthermore,' Elspeth says, ' how has the marriage been postponed twice ? ' We ken what the servants at the Spittal says to that, namely, that the young lady is no keen to take him, but Elspeth winna listen to sic arguments. She says either the earl had grown timid (as mony a man does), when the wedding-day drew near, or else his sister that keeps his house is mad at the thocht o' losing her place; but as for the young lady's being sweer, says Elspeth, ' an earl's an earl however auld he is, and a lassie's a lassie however young she is, and weel she kens you're never sure o' a man's no changing his mind about you till you're tied to him by law, after which it doesna so muckle matter whether he changes his mind about you or no.' Ay, there's a quirk in it some gait, dominie; but it's a deep water Elspeth canna bottom."

307

" It is," I agreed; " but you were to tell me what Birse told you of the disturbance at the Spittal."

" Ay, weel," he answered, " the post puts the wite o't on her little leddyship, as they call her, though she winna be a leddyship till the morn. All I can say is that if the earl was saft enough to do sic a thing out o' fondness for her, it's time he was married on her, so that he may come to his senses again. That's what I say; but Elspeth conters me, of course, and says she, ' If the young leddy was so careless o' insulting other folks' ancestors, it proves she has nane o' her ain; for them that has china plates themsels is the maist careful no to break the china plates of others.' "

" But what was the insult? Was Lauchlan dismissed? "

" Na, faags! It was waur than that. Dominie, you're dull in the uptake compared to Elspeth. I hadna telled her half the story afore she jaloused the rest. However, to begin again; there's great feasting and rejoicings gaen on at the Spittal the now, and also a banquet, which the post says is twa dinners in one. Weel, there's a curran Ogilvys among the guests, and it was them that egged on her little leddyship to make the daring proposal to the earl. What was the proposal? It was no less than that the twa pipers should be ordered to play ' The Bonny House o' Airlie.' Dominie, I wonder you can tak it so calm when you ken that's the Ogilvys sang, and that it's aimed at the clan o' Campbell."

"Pooh!" I said. "The Ogilvys and the Campbells used to be mortal enemies, but the feud has been long forgotten."

"Ay, I've heard tell," Waster Lunny said sceptically, "that Airlie and Argyle shakes hands now like Christians; but I'm thinking that's just afore the Queen. Dinna speak now, for I'm in the thick o't. Her little leddyship was all hinging in gold and jewels, the which winna be her ain till the morn; and she leans ower to the earl and whispers to him to get the pipers to play 'The Bonny House.' He wasna willing, for says he, 'There's Ogilvys at the table, and ane o' the pipers is a Campbell, and we'll better let sleeping dogs lie.' However, the Ogilvys lauched at his caution; and he was so infatuated wi' her little leddyship that he gae in, and he cried out to the pipers to strike up 'The Bonny House.'"

Waster Lunny pulled his chair nearer me and rested his hand on my knees.

"Dominie," he said in a voice that fell now and again into a whisper, "them looking on swears that when Lauchlan Campbell heard these monstrous orders his face became ugly and black, so that they kent in a jiffy what he would do. It's said a' body jumped back frae him in a sudden dread, except poor Angus, the other piper, wha was busy tuning up for 'The Bonny House.' Weel, Angus had got no farther in the tune than the first skirl when Lauchlan louped at him, and ripped up the startled crittur's pipes wi' his dirk. The pipes gae a roar o' agony like a stuck swine, and fell gasping on the floor. What happened next was that Lauchlan wi' his dirk handy for onybody that micht try to stop him, marched once round the table, playing ' The Campbells are coming,' and then straucht out o' the Spittal, his chest far afore him, and his head so weel back that he could see what was going on ahint. Frae the Spittal to here he never stopped that fearsome tune, and I'se warrant he's blawing away at it at this moment through the streets o' Thrums."

Waster Lunny was not in his usual spirits, or he would have repeated his story before he left me, for he had usually as much difficulty in coming to an end as in finding a beginning. The drouth was to him as serious a matter as death in the house, and as little to be forgotten for a lengthened period.

" There's to be a prayer-meeting for rain in the Auld Licht kirk the night," he told me as I escorted him as far as my side of the Quharity, now almost a dead stream, pitiable to see, " and I'm gaen; though I'm sweer to leave thae puir cattle o' mine. You should see how they look at me when I gie them mair o' that rotten grass to eat. It's eneuch to mak a man greet, for what richt hae I to keep kye when I canna meat them?"

Waster Lunny has said to me more than once that the great surprise of his life was when Elspeth was willing to take him. Many a time, however, I have seen that in him which might have made any weaver's daughter proud of such a man, and I saw it again when we came to the river side.

"I'm no ane o' thae farmers," he said truthfully, "that's aye girding at the weather, and Elspeth and me kens that we hae been dealt wi' bountifully since we took this farm wi' gey anxious hearts. That woman, dominie, is eneuch to put a brave face on a coward, and it's no langer syne than yestreen when I was sitting in the dumps, looking at the aurora borealis, which I canna but regard as a messenger o' woe, that she put her hand on my shoulder, and she says, 'Waster Lunny, twenty year syne we began life thegither wi' nothing but the claethes on our back, and an it please God we can begin it again, for I hae you and you hae me, and I'm no cast down if you're no.' Dominie, is there mony sic women in the warld as that?"

"Many a one," I said.

"Ay, man, it shamed me, for I hae a kind o' delight in angering Elspeth, just to see what she'll say. I could hae ta'en her on my knee at that minute, but the bairns was there, and so it wouldna

311

hae dune. But I cheered her up, for, after all, the
drouth canna put us so far back as we was twenty
years syne, unless it's true what my father said,
that the aurora borealis is the devil's rainbow. I
saw it sax times in July month, and it made me
shut my een. You was out admiring it, dominie,
but I can never forget that it was seen in the year
twelve just afore the great storm. I was only a
laddie then, but I mind how that awful wind
stripped a' the standing corn in the glen in less
time than we've been here at the water's edge. It
was called the deil's besom. My father's hinmost
words to me was, ' It's time eneuch to greet, laddie,
when you see the aurora borealis.' I mind he was
so complete ruined in an hour that he had to apply
for relief frae the poor's rates. Think o' that, and
him a proud man. He would tak' nothing till one
winter day when we was a' starving, and syne I
gaed wi' him to speir for't, and he telled me to
grip his hand ticht, so that the cauldness o' mine
micht gie him courage. They were doling out
the charity in the Town's House, and I had never
been in't afore. I canna look at it now without
thinking o' that day when me and my father gaed
up the stair thegither. Mr. Duthie was presiding
at the time, and he wasna muckle older than Mr.
Dishart is now. I mind he speired for proof that
we was needing, and my father couldna speak.
He just pointed at me. ' But you have a good

coat on your back yoursel',' Mr. Duthie said, for there were mony waiting, sair needing. ' It was lended him to come here,' I cried, and without a word my father opened the coat, and they saw he had nothing on aneath, and his skin blue wi' cauld. Dominie, Mr. Duthie handed him one shilling and saxpence, and my father's fingers closed greedily on't for a minute, and syne it fell to the ground. They put it back in his hand, and it slipped out again, and Mr. Duthie gave it back to him, saying, ' Are you so cauld as that ? ' But, oh, man, it wasna cauld that did it, but shame o' being on the rates. The blood a' ran to my father's head, and syne left it as quick, and he flung down the siller and walked out o' the Town's House wi' me running after him. We warstled through that winter, God kens how, and it's near a pleasure to me to think o't now, for, rain or no rain, I can never be reduced to sic straits again."

The farmer crossed the water without using the stilts which were no longer necessary, and I little thought, as I returned to the school-house, what terrible things were to happen before he could offer me his snuff-mull again. Serious as his talk had been it was neither of drouth nor of the incident at the Spittal that I sat down to think. My anxiety about Gavin came back to me until I was like a man imprisoned between walls of his own building. It may be that my presentiments of

313

that afternoon look gloomier now than they were, because I cannot return to them save over a night of agony, black enough to darken any time connected with it. Perhaps my spirits only fell as the wind rose, for wind ever takes me back to Harvie, and when I think of Harvie my thoughts are of the saddest. I know that I sat for some hours, now seeing Gavin pay the penalty of marrying the Egyptian, and again drifting back to my days with Margaret, until the wind took to playing tricks with me, so that I heard Adam Dishart enter our home by the sea every time the school-house door shook.

I became used to the illusion after starting several times, and thus when the door did open, about seven o'clock, it was only the wind rushing to my fire like a shivering dog that made me turn my head. Then I saw the Egyptian staring at me, and though her sudden appearance on my threshold was a strange thing, I forgot it in the whiteness of her face. She was looking at me like one who has asked a question of life or death, and stopped her heart for the reply.

"What is it?" I cried, and for a moment I believe I was glad she did not answer. She seemed to have told me already as much as I could bear.

"He has not heard," she said aloud in an expressionless voice, and, turning, would have slipped away without another word.

"Is any one dead?" I asked, seizing her hands and letting them fall, they were so clammy. She nodded, and trying to speak could not.

"He is dead," she said at last in a whisper. "Mr. Dishart is dead," and she sat down quietly.

At that I covered my face, crying, "God help Margaret!" and then she rose, saying fiercely, so that I drew back from her, "There is no Margaret; he only cared for me."

"She is his mother," I said hoarsely, and then she smiled to me, so that I thought her a harmless mad thing. "He was killed by a piper called Lauchlan Campbell," she said, looking up at me suddenly. "It was my fault."

"Poor Margaret!" I wailed.

"And poor Babbie," she entreated pathetically; "will no one say, 'Poor Babbie'?"

CHAPTER XXVII

FIRST JOURNEY OF THE DOMINIE TO THRUMS DURING THE TWENTY-FOUR HOURS

"How did it happen?" I asked more than once, but the Egyptian was only with me in the body, and she did not hear. I might have been talking to some one a mile away whom a telescope had drawn near my eyes.

When I put on my bonnet, however, she knew that I was going to Thrums, and she rose and walked to the door, looking behind to see that I followed.

"You must not come," I said harshly, but her hand started to her heart as if I had shot her, and I added quickly, "Come." We were already some distance on our way before I repeated my question.

"What matter how it happened?" she answered piteously, and they were words of which I felt the force. But when she said a little later, "I thought you would say it is not true," I took courage, and forced her to tell me all she knew. She sobbed while she spoke, if one may sob without tears.

"I heard of it at the Spittal," she said. "The news broke out suddenly there that the piper had quarrelled with some one in Thrums, and that in trying to separate them Mr. Dishart was stabbed. There is no doubt of its truth."

"We should have heard of it here," I said hopefully, "before the news reached the Spittal. It cannot be true."

"It was brought to the Spittal," she answered, "by the hill road."

Then my spirits sank again, for I knew that this was possible. There is a path, steep but short, across the hills between Thrums and the top of the glen, which Mr. Glendinning took frequently when he had to preach at both places on the same Sabbath. It is still called the Minister's Road.

"Yet if the earl had believed it he would have sent some one into Thrums for particulars," I said, grasping at such comfort as I could make.

"He does believe it," she answered. "He told me of it himself."

You see the Egyptian was careless of her secret now; but what was that secret to me? An hour ago it would have been much, and already it was not worth listening to. If she had begun to tell me why Lord Rintoul took a gypsy girl into his confidence I should not have heard her.

"I ran quickly," she said. "Even if a messenger was sent he might be behind me."

Was it her words or the tramp of a horse that made us turn our heads at that moment? I know not. But far back in a twist of the road we saw a horseman approaching at such a reckless pace that I thought he was on a runaway. We stopped instinctively, and waited for him, and twice he disappeared in hollows of the road, and then was suddenly tearing down upon us. I recognised in him young Mr. McKenzie, a relative of Rintoul, and I stretched out my arms to compel him to draw up. He misunderstood my motive, and was raising his whip threateningly, when he saw the Egyptian. It is not too much to say that he swayed in the saddle. The horse galloped on, though he had lost hold of the reins. He looked behind until he rounded a corner, and I never saw such amazement mixed with incredulity on a human face. For some minutes I expected to see him coming back, but when he did not I said wonderingly to the Egyptian—

" He knew you."

" Did he? " she answered indifferently, and I think we spoke no more until we were in Windyghoul. Soon we were barely conscious of each other's presence. Never since have I walked between the school-house and Thrums in so short a time, nor seen so little on the way.

In the Egyptian's eyes, I suppose, was a picture of Gavin lying dead; but if her grief had killed her thinking faculties, mine that was only less keen because I had been struck down once before, had set all the wheels of my brain in action. For it seemed to me that the hour had come when I must disclose myself to Margaret.

I had realised always that if such a necessity did arise it could only be caused by Gavin's premature death, or by his proving a bad son to her. Some may wonder that I could have looked calmly thus far into the possible, but I reply that the night of Adam Dishart's home-coming had made of me a man whom the future could not surprise again. Though I saw Gavin and his mother happy in our Auld Licht manse, that did not prevent my considering the contingencies which might leave her without a son. In the schoolhouse I had brooded over them as one may think over moves on a draught-board. It may have been idle, but it was done that I might know how to act best for Margaret if anything untoward occurred. The time for such action had come. Gavin's death had struck me hard, but it did not crush me. I was not unprepared. I was going to Margaret now.

What did I see as I walked quickly along the glen road, with Babbie silent by my side, and I doubt not pods of the broom cracking all around us? I saw myself entering the Auld Licht manse, where Margaret sat weeping over the body of Gavin, and there was none to break my coming to her, for none but she and I knew what had been.

I saw my Margaret again, so fragile now, so thin the wrists, her hair turned grey. No nearer could I go, but stopped at the door, grieving for her, and at last saying her name aloud.

I saw her raise her face, and look upon me for the first time for eighteen years. She did not scream at sight of me, for the body of her son lay between us, and bridged the gulf that Adam Dishart had made.

I saw myself draw near her reverently and say, "Margaret, he is dead, and that is why I have come back," and I saw her put her arms around my neck as she often did long ago.

But it was not to be. Never since that night at Harvie have I spoken to Margaret.

The Egyptian and I were come to Windyghoul before I heard her speak. She was not addressing me. Here Gavin and she had met first, and she was talking of that meeting to herself.

"It was there," I heard her say softly, as she gazed at the bush beneath which she had seen him shaking his fist at her on the night of the riots. A little farther on she stopped where a path from Windyghoul sets off for the well in the wood. She looked up it wistfully, and there I left her behind, and pressed on to the mud house to ask Nanny Webster if the minister was dead. Nanny's gate was swinging in the wind, but her door was shut, and for a moment I stood at it like a coward, afraid to enter and hear the worst.

The house was empty. I turned from it relieved, as if I had got a respite, and while I stood in the garden the Egyptian came to me shuddering, her twitching face asking the question that would not leave her lips.

" There is no one in the house," I said. " Nanny is perhaps at the well."

But the gypsy went inside, and pointing to the fire said, " It has been out for hours. Do you not see ? The murder has drawn every one into Thrums."

So I feared. A dreadful night was to pass before I knew that this was the day of the release of Sanders Webster, and that frail Nanny had walked into Tilliedrum to meet him at the prison gate.

Babbie sank upon a stool, so weak that I doubt whether she heard me tell her to wait there until my return. I hurried into Thrums, not by the hill, though it is the shorter way, but by the Roods, for I must hear all before I ventured to approach the manse. From Windyghoul to the top of the Roods it is a climb and then a steep descent. The road has no sooner reached its highest point than it begins to fall in the straight line of houses called the Roods, and thus I came upon a full view of the street at once. A cart was labouring up it. There were women sitting on stones at their doors, and girls playing at palaulays, and out of the house nearest me came a black figure. My eyes failed me; I was asking so much from them. They made him tall and short, and spare and stout, so that I knew it was Gavin, and yet, looking again, feared, but all the time, I think, I knew it was he.

CHAPTER XXVIII

THE HILL BEFORE DARKNESS FELL — SCENE OF THE IMPENDING CATASTROPHE

"You are better now?" I heard Gavin ask, presently.

He thought that having been taken ill suddenly I had waved to him for help, because he chanced to be near. With all my wits about me I might have left him in that belief, for rather would I have deceived him than had him wonder why his welfare seemed so vital to me. But I, who thought the capacity for being taken aback had gone from me, clung to his arm and thanked God audibly that he still lived. He did not tell me then how my agitation puzzled him, but led me kindly to the hill, where we could talk without listeners. By the time we reached it I was again wary, and I had told him what had brought me to Thrums, without mentioning how the story of his death reached my ears, or through whom.

"Mr. McKenzie," he said, interrupting me, "galloped all the way from the Spittal on the same errand. However, no one has been hurt much, except the piper himself."

Then he told me how the rumour arose.

" You know of the incident at the Spittal, and that Campbell marched off in high dudgeon? I understand that he spoke to no one between the Spittal and Thrums, but by the time he arrived here he was more communicative; yes, and thirstier. He was treated to drink in several publichouses by persons who wanted to hear his story, and by-and-by he began to drop hints of knowing something against the earl's bride. Do you know Rob Dow?"

" Yes," I answered, "and what you have done for him."

" Ah, sir!" he said, sighing, "for a long time I thought I was to be God's instrument in making a better man of Rob, but my power over him went long ago. Ten short months of the ministry takes some of the vanity out of a man."

Looking sideways at him I was startled by the unnatural brightness of his eyes. Unconsciously he had acquired the habit of pressing his teeth together in the pauses of his talk, shutting them on some woe that would proclaim itself, as men do who keep their misery to themselves."

" A few hours ago," he went on, "I heard Rob's voice in altercation as I passed the Bull tavern, and I had a feeling that if I failed with him so should I fail always throughout my ministry. I walked into the public-house, and stopped at the door of a room in which Dow and the piper were sitting drinking. I heard Rob saying, fiercely, 'If what you say about her is true, Highlandman, she's the woman I've been looking for this half year and mair; what is she like?' I guessed, from what I had been told of the piper, that they were speaking of the earl's bride, but Rob saw me and came to an abrupt stop, saying to his companion, 'Dinna say another word about her afore the minister.' Rob would have come away at once in answer to my appeal, but the piper was drunk and would not be silenced. 'I'll tell the minister about her, too,' he began. 'You dinna ken what you're doing,' Rob roared, and then, as if to save my ears from scandal at any cost, he struck Campbell a heavy blow on the mouth. I tried to intercept the blow, with the result that I fell, and then some one ran out of the tavern crying, 'He's killed!' The piper had been stunned, but the story went abroad that he had stabbed me for interfering with him. That is really all. Nothing, as you know, can overtake an untruth if it has a minute's start."

"Where is Campbell now?"

"Sleeping off the effect of the blow: but Dow has fled. He was terrified at the shouts of murder, and ran off up the West Town end. The doctor's dog-cart was standing at a door there and Rob jumped into it and drove off. They did not

325

chase him far, because he is sure to hear the truth soon, and then, doubtless, he will come back."

Though in a few hours we were to wonder at our denseness, neither Gavin nor I saw why Dow had struck the Highlander down rather than let him tell his story in the minister's presence. One moment's suspicion would have lit our way to the whole truth, but of the spring to all Rob's behaviour in the past eight months we were ignorant, and so to Gavin the Bull had only been the scene of a drunken brawl, while I forgot to think in the joy of finding him alive.

"I have a prayer-meeting for rain presently," Gavin said, breaking a picture that had just appeared unpleasantly before me of Babbie still in agony at Nanny's, "but before I leave you tell me why this rumour caused you such distress."

The question troubled me, and I tried to avoid it. Crossing the hill we had by this time drawn near a hollow called the Toad's-hole, then gay and noisy with a caravan of gypsies. They were those same wild Lindsays, for whom Gavin had searched Caddam one eventful night, and as I saw them crowding round their king, a man well known to me, I guessed what they were at.

"Mr. Dishart," I said abruptly, "would you like to see a gypsy marriage? One is taking place there just now. That big fellow is the king, and he is about to marry two of his people over the tongs. The ceremony will not detain us five minutes, though the rejoicings will go on all night."

I have been present at more than one gypsy wedding in my time, and at the wild, weird orgies that followed them, but what is interesting to such as I may not be for a minister's eyes, and, frowning at my proposal, Gavin turned his back upon the Toad's-hole. Then, as we recrossed the hill, to get away from the din of the camp, I pointed out to him that the report of his death had brought McKenzie to Thrums, as well as me.

" As soon as McKenzie heard I was not dead," he answered, " he galloped off to the Spittal, without even seeing me. I suppose he posted back to be in time for the night's rejoicings there. So you see, it was not solicitude for me that brought him. He came because a servant at the Spittal was supposed to have done the deed."

" Well, Mr. Dishart," I had to say, " why should I deny that I have a warm regard for you ? You have done brave work in our town."

" It has been little," he replied. " With God's help it will be more in future."

He meant that he had given time to his sad love affair that he owed to his people. Of seeing Babbie again I saw that he had given up hope. Instead of repining, he was devoting his whole soul to God's work. I was proud of him, and yet I grieved, for I could not think that God wanted him to bury his youth so soon.

"I had thought," he confessed to me, "that you were one of those who did not like my preaching."

"You were mistaken," I said, gravely. I dared not tell him that, except his mother, none would have sat under him so eagerly as I.

"Nevertheless," he said, "you were a member of the Auld Licht church in Mr. Carfrae's time, and you left it when I came."

"I heard your first sermon," I said.

"Ah," he replied. "I had not been long in Thrums before I discovered that if I took tea with any of my congregation and declined a second cup, they thought it a reflection on their brewing."

"You must not look upon my absence in that light," was all I could say. "There are reasons why I cannot come."

He did not press me further, thinking I meant that the distance was too great, though frailer folk than I walked twenty miles to hear him. We might have parted thus had we not wandered by chance to the very spot where I had met him and Babbie. There is a seat there now for those who lose their breath on the climb up, and so I have two reasons nowadays for not passing the place by.

We read each other's thoughts, and Gavin said calmly, "I have not seen her since that night. She disappeared as into a grave."

How could I answer when I knew that Babbie was dying for want of him, not half a mile away?

"You seemed to understand everything that night," he went on; "or if you did not, your thoughts were very generous to me."

In my sorrow for him I did not notice that we were moving on again, this time in the direction of Windyghoul.

"She was only a gypsy girl," he said, abruptly, and I nodded. "But I hoped," he continued, "that she would be my wife."

"I understood that," I said.

"There was nothing monstrous to you," he asked, looking me in the face, "in a minister's marrying a gypsy?"

I own that if I had loved a girl, however far below or above me in degree, I would have married her had she been willing to take me. But to Gavin I only answered, "These are matters a man must decide for himself."

"I had decided for myself," he said, emphatically.

"Yet," I said, wanting him to talk to me of Margaret, "in such a case one might have others to consider besides himself."

"A man's marriage," he answered, "is his own affair. I would have brooked no interference from my congregation."

I thought, " There is some obstinacy left in him still "; but aloud I said, " It was of your mother I was thinking."

"She would have taken Babbie to her heart," he said, with the fond conviction of a lover.

I doubted it, but I only asked, " Your mother knows nothing of her ? "

" Nothing," he rejoined. " It would be cruelty to tell my mother of her now that she is gone."

Gavin's calmness had left him, and he was striding quickly nearer to Windyghoul. I was in dread lest he should see the Egyptian at Nanny's door, yet to have turned him in another direction might have roused his suspicions. When we were within a hundred yards of the mud house, I knew that there was no Babbie in sight. We halved the distance and then I saw her at the open window. Gavin's eyes were on the ground, but she saw him. I held my breath, fearing that she would run out to him.

" You have never seen her since that night ? " Gavin asked me, without hope in his voice.

Had he been less hopeless he would have wondered why I did not reply immediately. I was looking covertly at the mud house, of which we were now within a few yards. Babbie's face had gone from the window, and the door remained shut. That she could hear every word we uttered now, I could not doubt. But she was hiding from the man for whom her soul longed. She was sacrificing herself for him.

"Never," I answered, notwithstanding my pity for the brave girl, and then while I was shaking lest he should go in to visit Nanny, I heard the echo of the Auld Licht bell.

"That calls me to the meeting for rain," Gavin said, bidding me good-night. I had acted for Margaret, and yet I had hardly the effrontery to take his hand. I suppose he saw sympathy in my face, for suddenly the cry broke from him —

"If I could only know that nothing evil had befallen her!"

Babbie heard him and could not restrain a heart-breaking sob.

"What was that?" he said, starting.

A moment I waited, to let her show herself if she chose. But the mud house was silent again.

"It was some boy in the wood," I answered.

"Good-bye," he said, trying to smile.

Had I let him go, here would have been the end of his love story, but that piteous smile unmanned me, and I could not keep the words back.

"She is in Nanny's house," I cried.

In another moment these two were together for weal or woe, and I had set off dizzily for the school-house, feeling now that I had been false to

Margaret, and again exulting in what I had done. By-and-by the bell stopped, and Gavin and Babbie regarded it as little as I heeded the burns now crossing the glen road noisily at places that had been dry two hours before.

CHAPTER XXIX

STORY OF THE EGYPTIAN

GOD gives us more than, were we not over-bold, we should dare to ask for, and yet how often (perhaps after saying "Thank God" so curtly that it is only a form of swearing) we are suppliants again within the hour. Gavin was to be satisfied if he were told that no evil had befallen her he loved, and all the way between the school-house and Windyghoul Babbie craved for no more than Gavin's life. Now they had got their desires; but do you think they were content?

The Egyptian had gone on her knees when she heard Gavin speak of her. It was her way of preventing herself from running to him. Then when she thought him gone, he opened the door. She rose and shrank back, but first she had stepped toward him with a glad cry. His disappointed arms met on nothing.

"You, too, heard that I was dead?" he said, thinking her strangeness but grief too sharply turned to joy.

There were tears in the word with which she

333

answered him, and he would have kissed her, but she defended her face with her hand.

"Babbie," he asked, beginning to fear that he had not sounded her deepest woe, "why have you left me all this time? You are not glad to see me now?"

"I was glad," she answered in a low voice, "to see you from the window, but I prayed to God not to let you see me."

She even pulled away her hand when he would have taken it. "No, no, I am to tell you everything now, and then——"

"Say that you love me first," he broke in, when a sob checked her speaking.

"No," she said, "I must tell you first what I have done, and then you will not ask me to say that. I am not a gypsy."

"What of that?" cried Gavin. "It was not because you were a gypsy that I loved you."

"That is the last time you will say you love me," said Babbie. "Mr. Dishart, I am to be married to-morrow."

She stopped, afraid to say more lest he should fall, but except that his arms twitched he did not move.

"I am to be married to Lord Rintoul," she went on. "Now you know who I am."

She turned from him, for his piercing eyes frightened her. Never again, she knew, would she see the love-light in them. He plucked him-self from the spot where he had stood looking at her, and walked to the window. When he wheeled round there was no anger on his face, only a pathetic wonder that he had been deceived so easily. It was at himself that he was smiling grimly rather than at her, and the change pained Babbie as no words could have hurt her. He sat down on a chair, and waited for her to go on.

"Don't look at me," she said, "and I will tell you everything." He dropped his eyes listlessly, and had he not asked her a question from time to time she would have doubted whether he heard her.

"After all," she said, "a gypsy dress is my birth-right, and so the Thrums people were scarcely wrong in calling me an Egyptian. It is a pity any one insisted on making me something differ-ent. I believe I could have been a good gypsy."

"Who were your parents?" Gavin asked, with-out looking up.

"You ask that," she said, "because you have a good mother. It is not a question that would oc-cur to me. My mother —— If she was bad may not that be some excuse for me? Ah, but I have no wish to excuse myself. Have you seen a gypsy cart with a sort of hammock swung beneath it in which gypsy children are carried about the country? If there are no children, the pots and

335

pans are stored in it. Unless the roads are rough it makes a comfortable cradle, and it was the only one I ever knew. Well, one day I suppose the road was rough, for I was capsized. I remember picking myself up after a little and running after the cart, but they did not hear my cries. I sat down by the roadside and stared after the cart until I lost sight of it. That was in England, and I was not three years old."

"But surely," Gavin said, "they came back to look for you?"

"So far as I know," Babbie answered hardly, "they did not come back. I have never seen them since. I think they were drunk. My only recollection of my mother is that she once took me to see the dead body of some gypsy who had been murdered. She told me to dip my hand in the blood, so that I could say I had done so when I became a woman. It was meant as a treat to me, and is the one kindness I am sure I got from her. Curiously enough, I felt the shame of her deserting me for many years afterwards. As a child I cried hysterically at thought of it; it pained me when I was at school in Edinburgh every time I saw the other girls writing home; I cannot think of it without a shudder, even now. It is what makes me worse than other women."

Her voice had altered, and she was speaking passionately.

" Sometimes," she continued, more gently, " I
try to think that my mother did come back for
me, and then went away because she heard I was
in better hands than hers. It was Lord Rintoul
who found me, and I owe everything to him.
You will say that he has no need to be proud of
me. He took me home on his horse, and paid his
gardener's wife to rear me. She was Scotch, and
that is why I can speak two languages. It was he,
too, who sent me to school in Edinburgh."

" He has been very kind to you," said Gavin,
who would have preferred to dislike the earl.

" So kind," answered Babbie, " that now he is
to marry me. But do you know why he has done
all this ? "

Now again she was agitated, and spoke indignantly.

" It is all because I have a pretty face," she said,
her bosom rising and falling. " Men think of
nothing else. He had no pity for the deserted
child. I knew that while I was yet on his horse.
When he came to the gardener's afterwards it was
not to give me some one to love, it was only to
look upon what was called my beauty; I was
merely a picture to him, and even the gardener's
children knew it and sought to terrify me by saying, ' You are losing your looks; the earl will not
care for you any more.' Sometimes he brought
his friends to see me, ' because I was such a lovely

child,' and if they did not agree with him on that point he left without kissing me. Throughout my whole girlhood I was taught nothing but to please him, and the only way to do that was to be pretty. It was the only virtue worth striving for; the others were never thought of when he asked how I was getting on. Once I had fever and nearly died, yet this knowledge that my face was everything was implanted in me so that my fear lest he should think me ugly when I recovered terrified me into hysterics. I dream still that I am in that fever and all my fears return. He did think me ugly when he saw me next. I remember the incident so well still. I had run to him, and he was lifting me up to kiss me when he saw that my face had changed. 'What a cruel disappointment,' he said, and turned his back on me. I had given him a child's love until then, but from that day I was hard and callous."

" And when was it you became beautiful again ? " Gavin asked, by no means in the mind to pay compliments.

" A year passed," she continued, " before I saw him again. In that time he had not asked for me once, and the gardener had kept me out of charity. It was by an accident that we met, and at first he did not know me. Then he said, ' Why, Babbie, I believe you are to be a beauty after all ! ' I hated him for that, and stalked away from him, but he called after me, 'Bravo! she walks like a queen;' and it was because I walked like a queen that he sent me to an Edinburgh school. He used to come to see me every year, and as I grew up the girls called me Lady Rintoul. He was not fond of me; he is not fond of me now. He would as soon think of looking at the back of a picture as at what I am apart from my face, but he dotes on it, and is to marry it. Is that love? Long before I left school, which was shortly before you came to Thrums, he had told his sister that he was determined to marry me, and she hated me for it, making me as uncomfortable as she could, so that I almost looked forward to the marriage because it would be such a humiliation to her."

In admitting this she looked shamefacedly at Gavin, and then went on —

" It is humiliating him too. I understand him. He would like not to want to marry me, for he is ashamed of my origin, but he cannot help it. It is this feeling that has brought him here, so that the marriage may take place where my history is not known."

" The secret has been well kept," Gavin said, " for they have failed to discover it even in Thrums."

" Some of the Spittal servants suspect it, nevertheless," Babbie answered, " though how much they know I cannot say. He has not a servant now, either here or in England, who knew me as a child. The gardener who befriended me was sent away long ago. Lord Rintoul looks upon me as a disgrace to him that he cannot live without."

"I dare say he cares for you more than you think," Gavin said gravely.

"He is infatuated about my face, or the pose of my head, or something of that sort," Babbie said bitterly, "or he would not have endured me so long. I have twice had the wedding postponed, chiefly, I believe, to enrage my natural enemy, his sister, who is as much aggravated by my reluctance to marry him as by his desire to marry me. However, I also felt that imprisonment for life was approaching as the day drew near, and I told him that if he did not defer the wedding I should run away. He knows I am capable of it, for twice I ran away from school. If his sister only knew that!"

For a moment it was the old Babbie Gavin saw; but her glee was short-lived, and she resumed sedately —

"They were kind to me at school, but the life was so dull and prim that I ran off in a gypsy dress of my own making. That is what it is to have gypsy blood in one. I was away for a week the first time, wandering the country alone, telling fortunes, dancing and singing in woods and sleeping in barns. I am the only woman in the world well brought up who is not afraid of mice or rats. That is my gypsy blood again. After that wild week I went back to the school of my own will, and no one knows of the escapade but my school-mistress and Lord Rintoul. The second time, however, I was detected singing in the street, and then my future husband was asked to take me away. Yet Miss Feversham cried when I left, and told me that I was the nicest girl she knew, as well as the nastiest. She said she should love me as soon as I was not one of her boarders."

"And then you came to the Spittal?"

"Yes; and Lord Rintoul wanted me to say I was sorry for what I had done, but I told him I need not say that, for I was sure to do it again. As you know, I have done it several times since then; and though I am a different woman since I knew you, I dare say I shall go on doing it at times all my life. You shake your head because you do not understand. It is not that I make up my mind to break out in that way; I may not have had the least desire to do it for weeks, and then suddenly, when I am out riding, or at dinner, or at a dance, the craving to be a gypsy again is so strong that I never think of resisting it; I would risk my life to gratify it. Yes, whatever my life in the future is to be, I know that must be part of it. I used to pretend at the Spittal that I had gone to bed, and then escape by the window. I was mad with glee at those times, but I always re-turned before morning, except once, the last time I saw you, when I was away for nearly twenty-four hours. Lord Rintoul was so glad to see me come back then, that he almost forgave me for going away. There is nothing more to tell except that on the night of the riot it was not my gypsy na-ture that brought me to Thrums, but a desire to save the poor weavers. I had heard Lord Rintoul and the sheriff discussing the contemplated raid. I have hidden nothing from you. In time, per-haps, I shall have suffered sufficiently for all my wickedness."

Gavin rose weariedly, and walked through the mud house looking at her.

" This is the end of it all," he said harshly, com-ing to a standstill. " I loved you, Babbie."

" No," she answered, shaking her head. " You never knew me until now, and so it was not me you loved. I know what you thought I was, and I will try to be it now."

" If you had only told me this before," the min-ister said sadly, " it might not have been too late."

" I only thought you like all the other men I knew," she replied, " until the night I came to the manse. It was only my face you admired at first."

" No, it was never that," Gavin said with such conviction that her mouth opened in alarm to ask him if he did not think her pretty. She did not speak, however, and he continued, " You must have known that I loved you from the first night."

" No; you only amused me," she said, like one determined to stint nothing of the truth. " Even at the well I laughed at your vows."

This wounded Gavin afresh, wretched as her story had made him, and he said tragically, " You have never cared for me at all."

" Oh, always, always," she answered, " since I knew what love was; and it was you who taught me."

Even in his misery he held his head high with pride. At least she did love him.

" And then," Babbie said, hiding her face, " I could not tell you what I was because I knew you would loathe me. I could only go away."

She looked at him forlornly through her tears, and then moved toward the door. He had sunk upon a stool, his face resting on the table, and it was her intention to slip away unnoticed. But he heard the latch rise, and jumping up, said sharply, " Babbie, I cannot give you up."

She stood in tears, swinging the door unconsciously with her hand.

" Don't say that you love me still," she cried; and then, letting her hand fall from the door, added imploringly, " Oh, Gavin, do you ? "

343

CHAPTER XXX

THE MEETING FOR RAIN

MEANWHILE the Auld Lichts were in church, waiting for their minister, and it was a full meeting, because nearly every well in Thrums had been scooped dry by anxious palms. Yet not all were there to ask God's rain for themselves. Old Charles Yuill was in his pew, after dreaming thrice that he would break up with the drouth; and Bell Christison had come, though her man lay dead at home, and she thought it could matter no more to her how things went in the world.

You, who do not love that little congregation, would have said that they were waiting placidly. But probably so simple a woman as Meggy Rattray could have deceived you into believing that because her eyes were downcast she did not notice who put the threepenny-bit in the plate. A few men were unaware that the bell was working overtime, most of them farmers with their eyes on the windows, but all the women at least were wondering. They knew better, however, than to bring their thoughts to their faces, and none sought to

344

catch another's eye. The men-folk looked heavily
at their hats in the seats in front. Even when
Hendry Munn, instead of marching to the pulpit
with the big Bible in his hands, came as far as the
plate and signed to Peter Tosh, elder, that he was
wanted in the vestry, you could not have guessed
how every woman there, except Bell Christison,
wished she was Peter Tosh. Peter was so taken
aback that he merely gaped at Hendry, until suddenly he knew that his five daughters were furious with him, when he dived for his hat and
staggered to the vestry with his mouth open. His
boots cheeped all the way, but no one looked up.

"I hadna noticed the minister was lang in coming," Waster Lunny told me afterwards, "but Elspeth noticed it, and with a quickness that baffles
me she saw I was thinking o' other things. So
she let out her foot at me. I gae a low cough to
let her ken I wasna sleeping, but in a minute out
goes her foot again. Ay, syne I thocht I might
hae dropped my hanky into Snecky Hobart's pew,
but no, it was in my tails. Yet her hand was on
the board, and she was working her fingers in a
way that I kent meant she would like to shake
me. Next I looked to see if I was sitting on her
frock, the which tries a woman sair, but I wasna.
'Does she want to change Bibles wi' me?' I wondered; 'or is she sliding yont a peppermint to
me?' It was neither, so I edged as far frae her as

I could gang. Weel, would you credit it, I saw her body coming nearer me inch by inch, though she was looking straucht afore her, till she was within kick o' me, and then out again goes her foot. At that, dominie, I lost patience, and I whispered, fierce-like, 'Keep your foot to yoursel', you limmer!' Ay, her intent, you see, was to waken me to what was gaen on, but I couldna be expected to ken that."

In the vestry Hendry Munn was now holding counsel with three elders, of whom the chief was Lang Tammas.

"The laddie I sent to the manse," Hendry said, "canna be back this five minutes, and the question is how we're to fill up that time. I'll ring no langer, for the bell has been in a passion ever since a quarter-past eight. It's as sweer to clang past the quarter as a horse to gallop by its stable."

"You could gang to your box and gie out a psalm, Tammas," suggested John Spens.

"And would a psalm sung wi' sic an object," retorted the precentor, "mount higher, think you, than a bairn's kite? I'll insult the Almighty to screen no minister."

"You're screening him better by standing whaur you are," said the imperturbable Hendry, "for as lang as you dinna show your face they'll think it may be you that's missing instead o' Mr. Dishart."

Indeed, Gavin's appearance in church without

346

the precentor would have been as surprising as Tammas's without the minister. As certainly as the shutting of a money-box is followed by the turning of the key, did the precentor walk stiffly from the vestry to his box a toll of the bell in front of the minister. Tammas's halfpenny rang in the plate as Gavin passed T'nowhead's pew, and Gavin's sixpence with the snapping-to of the precentor's door. The two men might have been connected by a string that tightened at ten yards.

"The congregation ken me ower weel," Tammas said, "to believe I would keep the Lord waiting."

"And they are as sure o' Mr. Dishart," rejoined Spens, with spirit, though he feared the precentor on Sabbaths and at prayer-meetings. "You're a hard man."

"I speak the blunt truth," Whamond answered.

"Ay," said Spens, "and to tak' credit for that may be like blawing that you're ower honest to wear claethes."

Hendry, who had gone to the door, returned now with the information that Mr. Dishart had left the manse two hours ago to pay visits, meaning to come to the prayer-meeting before he returned home.

"There's a quirk in this, Hendry," said Tosh. "Was it Mistress Dishart the laddie saw?"

"No," Hendry replied. "It was Jean. She

347

canna get to the meeting because the mistress is nervous in the manse by herself; and Jean didna like to tell her that he's missing, for fear o' alarming her. What are we to do now?"

"He's an unfaithful shepherd," cried the precentor, while Hendry again went out. "I see it written on the walls."

"I dinna," said Spens doggedly.

"Because," retorted Tammas, "having eyes you see not."

"Tammas, I aye thocht you was fond o' Mr. Dishart."

"If my right eye were to offend me," answered the precentor, "I would pluck it out. I suppose you think, and baith o' you farmers too, that there's no necessity for praying for rain the nicht? You'll be content, will ye, if Mr. Dishart just drops in to the kirk some day accidental-like, and offers up a bit prayer?"

"As for the rain," Spens said, triumphantly, "I wouldna wonder though it's here afore the minister. You canna deny, Peter Tosh, that there's been a smell o' rain in the air this twa hours back."

"John," Peter said agitatedly, "dinna speak so confidently. I've kent it," he whispered, "since the day turned; but it wants to tak' us by surprise, lad, and so I'm no letting on."

"See that you dinna make an idol o' the rain," thundered Whamond. "Your thochts is no wi'

Him, but wi' the clouds; and whaur your thochts are, there will your prayers stick also."

" If you saw my lambs," Tosh began; and then, ashamed of himself, said, looking upwards, " He holds the rain in the hollow of His hand."

" And He's closing His neive ticht on't again," said the precentor solemnly. " Hearken to the wind rising."

" God help me ! " cried Tosh, wringing his hands. " Is it fair, think you," he said, passionately addressing the sky, " to show your wrath wi' Mr. Dishart by ruining my neeps ? "

" You were richt, Tammas Whamond," Spens said, growing hard as he listened to the wind, " the sanctuary o' the Lord has been profaned this nicht by him wha should be the chief pillar o' the building."

They were lowering brows that greeted Hendry when he returned to say that Mr. Dishart had been seen last on the hill with the Glen Quharity dominie.

" Some thinks," said the kirk-officer, " that he's awa hunting for Rob Dow."

" Nothing'll excuse him," replied Spens, " short o' his having fallen over the quarry."

Hendry's was usually a blank face, but it must have looked troubled now, for Tosh was about to say, " Hendry, you're keeping something back," when the precentor said it before him.

" Wi' that story o' Mr. Dishart's murder, no

many hours auld yet," the kirk-officer replied eva-sively, " we should be wary o' trusting gossip."

" What hae you heard ? "

" It's through the town," Hendry answered, "that a woman was wi' the dominie."

" A woman ! " cried Tosh. " The woman there's been sic talk about in connection wi' the minis-ter ? Whaur are they now ? "

" It's no kent, but — the dominie was seen goin' hame by himsel'."

" Leaving the minister and her thegither," cried the three men at once.

" Hendry Munn," Tammas said sternly, " there's mair about this; wha is the woman ? "

" They are liars," Hendry answered, and shut his mouth tight.

" Gie her a name, I say," the precentor ordered, " or, as chief elder of this kirk, supported by mair than half o' the Session, I command you to lift your hat and go."

Hendry gave an appealing look to Tosh and Spens, but the precentor's solemnity had cowed them.

" They say, then," he answered sullenly, " that it's the Egyptian. Yes, and I believe they ken."

The two farmers drew back from this statement incredulously; but Tammas Whamond jumped at the kirk-officer's throat, and some who were in the church that night say they heard Hendry

350

scream. Then the precentor's fingers relaxed their grip, and he tottered into the middle of the room.

" Hendry," he pleaded, holding out his arms pathetically, "tak' back these words. Oh, man, have pity, and tak' them back."

But Hendry would not, and then Lang Tammas's mouth worked convulsively, and he sobbed, crying, "Nobody kent it, but mair than mortal son, O God, did I love the lad!"

So seldom in a lifetime had any one seen into this man's heart that Spens said, amazed —

" Tammas, Tammas Whamond, it's no like you to break down."

The rusty door of Whamond's heart swung to.

" Who broke down ?" he asked fiercely. " Let no member of this Session dare to break down till his work be done."

" What work ?" Tosh said uneasily. " We canna interfere."

" I would rather resign," Spens said, but shook when Whamond hurled these words at him —

" ' And Jesus said unto him, No man, having put his hand to the plow and looking back, is fit for the kingdom of God.' "

" It mayna be true," Hendry said eagerly.

" We'll soon see."

" He would gie her up," said Tosh.

" Peter Tosh," answered Whamond sternly, " I call upon you to dismiss the congregation."

" Should we no rather haud the meeting our-sel's ? "

" We have other work afore us," replied the precentor.

" But what can I say ? " Tosh asked nervously. " Should I offer up a prayer ? "

" I warn you all," broke in Hendry, " that though the congregation is sitting there quietly, they'll be tigers for the meaning o' this as soon as they're in the street."

" Let no ontruth be telled them," said the pre-centor. " Peter Tosh, do your duty. John Spens, remain wi' me."

The church emptied silently, but a buzz of ex-citement arose outside. Many persons tried to enter the vestry, but were ordered away, and when Tosh joined his fellow-elders the people were col-lecting in animated groups in the square, or scat-tering through the wynds for news.

" And now," said the precentor, " I call upon the three o' you to come wi' me. Hendry Munn, you gang first."

" I maun bide ahint," Hendry said, with a sud-den fear, " to lock up the kirk."

" I'll lock up the kirk," Whamond answered harshly.

" You maun gie me the keys, though," entreated the kirk-officer.

" I'll take care o' the keys," said Whamond.

" I maun hae them," Hendry said, " to open the kirk on Sabbath."

The precentor locked the doors, and buttoned up the keys in his trousers pocket.

" Wha kens," he said in a voice of steel, " that the kirk'll be open next Sabbath ? "

" Hae some mercy on him, Tammas," Spens implored.   " He's no twa-and-twenty."

" Wha kens," continued the precentor, " but that the next time this kirk is opened will be to preach it toom ? "

" What road do we tak' ? "

" The road to the hill, whaur he was seen last."

CHAPTER XXXI

VARIOUS BODIES CONVERGING ON THE HILL

It would be coming on for a quarter-past nine, and a misty night, when I reached the school-house, and I was so weary of mind and body that I sat down without taking off my bonnet. I had left the door open, and I remember listlessly watching the wind making a target of my candle, but never taking a sufficiently big breath to do more than frighten it. From this lethargy I was roused by the sound of wheels.

In the daytime our glen road leads to many parts, but in the night only to the doctor's. Then the gallop of a horse makes farmers start up in bed and cry, " Who's ill? " I went to my door and listened to the trap coming swiftly down the lonely glen, but I could not see it, for there was a trailing scarf of mist between the school-house and the road. Presently I heard the swish of the wheels in water, and so learned that they were crossing the ford to come to me. I had been unstrung by the events of the evening, and fear at once pressed thick upon me that this might be a sequel to them, as indeed it was.

While still out of sight the trap stopped, and I heard some one jump from it. Then came this conversation, as distinct as though it had been spoken into my ear :—

"Can you see the school-house now, McKenzie?"

"I am groping for it, Rintoul. The mist seems to have made off with the path."

"Where are you, McKenzie? I have lost sight of you."

It was but a ribbon of mist, and as these words were spoken McKenzie broke through it. I saw him, though to him I was only a stone at my door.

"I have found the house, Rintoul," he shouted, "and there is a light in it, so that the fellow has doubtless returned."

"Then wait a moment for me."

"Stay where you are, Rintoul, I entreat you, and leave him to me. He may recognise you."

"No, no, McKenzie, I am sure he never saw me before. I insist on accompanying you."

"Your excitement, Rintoul, will betray you. Let me go alone. I can question him without rousing his suspicions. Remember, she is only a gypsy to him."

"He will learn nothing from me. I am quite calm now."

"Rintoul, I warn you your manner will betray

355

you, and to-morrow it will be roared through the countryside that your bride ran away from the Spittal in a gypsy dress, and had to be brought back by force."

The altercation may have lasted another minute, but the suddenness with which I learned Babbie's secret had left my ears incapable of learning more. I daresay the two men started when they found me at my door, but they did not remember, as few do remember who have the noisy day to forget it in, how far the voice carries in the night.

They came as suddenly on me as I on them, for though they had given unintentional notice of their approach, I had lost sight of the speakers in their amazing words. Only a moment did young McKenzie's anxiety to be spokesman give me to regard Lord Rintoul. I saw that he was a thin man and tall, straight in the figure, but his head begun to sink into his shoulders and not very steady on them. His teeth had grip of his under-lip, as if this was a method of controlling his agitation, and he was opening and shutting his hands restlessly. He had a dog with him which I was to meet again.

"Well met, Mr. Ogilvy," said McKenzie, who knew me slightly, having once acted as judge at a cock-fight in the school-house. "We were afraid we should have to rouse you."

"You will step inside?" I asked awkwardly,

and while I spoke I was wondering how long it would be before the earl's excitement broke out.

" It is not necessary," McKenzie answered hurriedly. " My friend and I (this is Mr. McClure) have been caught in the mist without a lamp, and we thought you could perhaps favour us with one."

" Unfortunately I have nothing of the kind," I said, and the state of mind I was in is shown by my answering seriously.

" Then we must wish you a good-night and manage as best we can," he said; and then before he could touch, with affected indifference, on the real object of their visit, the alarmed earl said angrily, " McKenzie, no more of this."

" No more of this delay, do you mean, McClure ? " asked McKenzie, and then turning to me said, " By the way, Mr. Ogilvy, I think this is our second meeting to-night. I met you on the road a few hours ago with your wife. Or was it your daughter ? "

" It was neither, Mr. McKenzie," I answered, with the calmness of one not yet recovered from a shock. " It was a gypsy girl."

" Where is she now ? " cried Rintoul feverishly; but McKenzie, speaking loudly at the same time, tried to drown his interference as one obliterates writing by writing over it.

" A strange companion for a schoolmaster," he said. " What became of her ? "

357

"I left her near Caddam Wood," I replied, "but she is probably not there now."

"Ah, they are strange creatures, these gypsies," he said, casting a warning look at the earl. "Now I wonder where she had been bound for?"

"There is a gypsy encampment on the hill," I answered, though I cannot say why.

"She is there!" exclaimed Rintoul, and was done with me.

"I daresay," McKenzie said, indifferently. "However, it is nothing to us. Good-night, sir."

The earl had started for the trap, but McKenzie's salute reminded him of a forgotten courtesy, and, despite his agitation, he came back to apologise. I admired him for this. Then my thoughtlessness must needs mar all.

"Good-night, Mr. McKenzie," I said. "Good-night, Lord Rintoul."

I had addressed him by his real name. Never a turnip fell from a bumping, laden cart, and the driver more unconscious of it, than I that I had dropped that word. I re-entered the house, but had not reached my chair when McKenzie's hand fell roughly on me, and I was swung round.

"Mr. Ogilvy," he said, the more savagely I doubt not because his passions had been chained so long, "you know more than you would have us think. Beware, sir, of recognising that gypsy should you ever see her again in different attire.

I advise you to have forgotten this night when you waken to-morrow morning."

With a menacing gesture he left me, and I sank into a chair, glad to lose sight of the glowering eyes with which he had pinned me to the wall. I did not hear the trap cross the ford and renew its journey. When I looked out next, the night had fallen very dark, and the glen was so deathly in its drowsiness that I thought not even the cry of murder could tear its eyes open.

The earl and McKenzie would be some distance still from the hill when the office-bearers had scoured it in vain for their minister. The gypsies, now dancing round their fires to music that, on ordinary occasions, Lang Tammas would have stopped by using his fists to the glory of God, had seen no minister, they said, and disbelieved in the existence of the mysterious Egyptian.

" Liars they are to trade," Spens declared to his companions, " but now and again they speak truth, like a standing clock, and I'm beginning to think the minister's lassie was invented in the square."

" Not so," said the precentor, " for we saw her oursel's a short year syne, and Hendry Munn there allows there's townsfolk that hae passed her in the glen mair recently."

" I only allowed," Hendry said cautiously, " that some sic talk had shot up sudden-like in the town. Them that pretends they saw her says that she joukit quick out o' sicht."

"Ay, and there's another quirk in that," responded the suspicious precentor.

" I'se uphaud the minister's sitting in the manse in his slippers by this time," Hendry said.

" I'm willing," replied Whamond, " to gang back and speir, or to search Caddam next; but let the matter drop I winna, though I ken you're a' awid to be hame now."

" And naturally," retorted Tosh, " for the nicht's coming on as black as pick, and by the time we're at Caddam, we'll no even see the trees."

Toward Caddam, nevertheless, they advanced, hearing nothing but a distant wind and the whish of their legs in the broom.

" Whaur's John Spens?" Hendry said suddenly.

They turned back, and found Spens rooted to the ground, as a boy becomes motionless when he thinks he is within arm's reach of a nest, and the bird sitting on the eggs.

" What do you see, man?" Hendry whispered.

" As sure as death," answered Spens, awe-struck, " I felt a drap o' rain."

" It's no rain we're here to look for," said the precentor.

" Peter Tosh," cried Spens, " it was a drap! Oh, Peter! how are you looking at me so queer, Peter, when you should be thanking the Lord for the promise that's in that drap?"

"Come away," Whamond said, impatiently; but Spens answered, "No till I've offered up a prayer for the promise that's in that drap. Peter Tosh, you've forgotten to take off your bonnet."

"Think twice, John Spens," gasped Tosh, "afore you pray for rain this nicht."

The others thought him crazy, but he went on, with a catch in his voice :—

"I felt a drap o' rain mysel', just afore it came on dark so hurried, and my first impulse was to wish that I could carry that drap about wi' me, and look at it. But, John Spens, when I looked up I saw sic a change running ower the sky that I thocht hell had taen the place o' heaven, and that there was waterspouts gathering therein for the drowning o' the world."

"There's no water in hell," the precentor said grimly.

"Genesis ix.," said Spens, "verses 8 to 17. Ay but, Peter, you've startled me, and I'm thinking we should be stepping hame. Is that a licht?"

"It'll be in Nanny Webster's," Hendry said, after they had all regarded the light.

"I never heard that Nanny needed a candle to licht her to her bed," the precentor muttered.

"She was awa to meet Sanders the day as he came out o' the Tilliedrum gaol," Spens remembered, "and I daresay the licht means they're hame again."

"It's well kent——" began Hendry, and would have recalled his words.

"Hendry Munn," cried the precentor, "if you hae minded onything that may help us, out wi't."

"I was just minding," the kirk-officer answered reluctantly, "that Nanny allows it's Mr. Dishart that has been keeping her frae the poorhouse. You canna censure him for that, Tammas."

"Can I no?" retorted Whamond. "What business has he to befriend a woman that belongs to another denomination? I'll see to the bottom o' that this nicht. Lads, follow me to Nanny's, and dinna be surprised if we find baith the minister and the Egyptian there."

They had not advanced many yards when Spens jumped to the side, crying, "Be wary, that's no the wind; it's a machine!"

Immediately the doctor's dog-cart was close to them, with Rob Dow for its only occupant. He was driving slowly, or Whamond could not have escaped the horse's hoofs.

"Is that you, Rob Dow?" said the precentor sourly. "I tell you, you'll be gaoled for stealing the doctor's machine."

"The Hielandman wasna muckle hurt, Rob," Hendry said, more good-naturedly.

"I ken that," replied Rob, scowling at the four

of them. "What are you doing here on sic a nicht?"

"Do you see anything strange in the nicht, Rob?" Tosh asked apprehensively.

"It's setting to rain," Dow replied. "I dinna see it, but I feel it."

"Ay," said Tosh, eagerly, "but will it be a saft, cowdie sweet ding-on?"

"Let the heavens open if they will," interposed Spens recklessly. "I would swap the drouth for rain, though it comes down in a sheet as in the year twelve."

"And like a sheet it'll come," replied Dow, "and the deil'll blaw it about wi' his biggest bellowses."

Tosh shivered, but Whamond shook him roughly, saying —

"Keep your oaths to yoursel', Rob Dow, and tell me, hae you seen Mr. Dishart?"

"I hinna," Rob answered curtly, preparing to drive on.

"Nor the lassie they call the Egyptian?"

Rob leaped from the dog-cart, crying, "What does that mean?"

"Hands off," said the precentor, retreating from him. "It means that Mr. Dishart neglected the prayer-meeting this nicht to philander after that heathen woman."

"We're no sure o't, Tammas," remonstrated the kirk-officer. Dow stood quite still. "I believe

Rob kens it's true," Hendry added sadly, "or he would hae flown at your throat, Tammas Whamond, for saying these words."

Even this did not rouse Dow.

"Rob doesna worship the minister as he used to do," said Spens.

"And what for no?" cried the precentor. "Rob Dow, is it because you've found out about this woman?"

"You're a pack o' liars," roared Rob, desperately, "and if you say again that ony wandering hussy has haud o' the minister, I'll let you see whether I can loup at throats."

"You'll swear by the Book," asked Whamond, relentlessly, "that you've seen neither o' them this nicht, nor them thegither at any time?"

"I so swear by the Book," answered poor loyal Rob. "But what makes you look for Mr. Dishart here?" he demanded, with an uneasy look at the light in the mud house.

"Go hame," replied the precentor, "and deliver up the machine you stole, and leave this Session to do its duty. John, we maun fathom the meaning o' that licht."

Dow started, and was probably at that moment within an ace of felling Whamond.

"I'll come wi' you," he said, hunting in his mind for a better way of helping Gavin.

They were at Nanny's garden, but in the darkness

364

Whamond could not find the gate. Rob climbed
the paling, and was at once lost sight of. Then
they saw his head obscure the window. They did
not, however, hear the groan that startled Babbie.

"There's nobody there," he said, coming back,
"but Nanny and Sanders. You'll mind Sanders
was to be freed the day."

"I'll go in and see Sanders," said Hendry, but
the precentor pulled him back, saying, "You'll do
nothing o' the kind, Hendry Munn; you'll come
awa wi' me now to the manse."

"It's mair than me and Peter'll do, then," said
Spens, who had been consulting with the other
farmer. "We're gaun as straucht hame as the
darkness'll let us."

With few more words the Session parted, Spens
and Tosh setting off for their farms, and Hendry
accompanying the precentor. No one will ever
know where Dow went. I can fancy him, however, returning to the wood, and there drawing
rein. I can fancy his mind made up to watch the
mud house until Gavin and the gypsy separated,
and then pounce upon her. I daresay his whole
plot could be condensed into a sentence, "If she's
got rid o' this nicht, we may cheat the Session
yet." But this is mere surmise. All I know is,
that he waited near Nanny's house, and by-and-by
heard another trap coming up Windyghoul. That
was just before the ten o'clock bell began to ring.

CHAPTER XXXII

LEADING SWIFTLY TO THE APPALLING MARRIAGE

THE little minister bowed his head in assent when Babbie's cry, " Oh, Gavin, do you ? " leapt in front of her unselfish wish that he should care for her no more.

" But that matters very little now," he said.

She was his to do with as he willed; and, perhaps, the joy of knowing herself loved still, begot a wild hope that he would refuse to give her up. If so, these words laid it low, but even the sentence they passed upon her could not kill the self-respect that would be hers henceforth. " That matters very little now," the man said, but to the woman it seemed to matter more than anything else in the world.

Throughout the remainder of this interview, until the end came, Gavin never faltered. His duty and hers lay so plainly before him that there could be no straying from it. Did Babbie think him strangely calm ? At the Glen Quharity gathering I once saw Rob Angus lift a boulder with such apparent ease that its weight was discredited, until the cry arose that the effort had dislocated his arm. Perhaps Gavin's quietness deceived the Egyptian similarly. Had he stamped, she might have understood better what he suffered, standing there on the hot embers of his passion.

"We must try to make amends now," he said gravely, "for the wrong we have done."

"The wrong I have done," she said, correcting him. "You will make it harder for me if you blame yourself. How vile I was in those days!"

"Those days," she called them; they seemed so far away.

"Do not cry, Babbie," Gavin replied, gently. "He knew what you were, and why, and He pities you. 'For His anger endureth but a moment: in His favour is life: weeping may endure for a night, but joy cometh in the morning.'"

"Not to me."

"Yes, to you," he answered. "Babbie, you will return to the Spittal now, and tell Lord Rintoul everything."

"If you wish it."

"Not because I wish it, but because it is right. He must be told that you do not love him."

"I never pretended to him that I did," Babbie said, looking up. "Oh," she added, with emphasis, "he knows that. He thinks me incapable of caring for any one."

"And that is why he must be told of me," Gavin replied. "You are no longer the woman you were, Babbie, and you know it, and I know it, but he does not know it. He shall know it before he decides whether he is to marry you."

Babbie looked at Gavin, and wondered he did not see that this decision lay with him.

"Nevertheless," she said, "the wedding will take place to-morrow; if it did not, Lord Rintoul would be the scorn of his friends."

"If it does," the minister answered, "he will be the scorn of himself. Babbie, there is a chance."

"There is no chance," she told him. "I shall be back at the Spittal without any one's knowing of my absence, and when I begin to tell him of you, he will tremble, lest it means my refusal to marry him; when he knows it does not, he will wonder only why I told him anything."

"He will ask you to take time——"

"No, he will ask me to put on my wedding-dress. You must not think anything else possible."

"So be it, then," Gavin said firmly.

"Yes, it will be better so," Babbie answered, and then, seeing him misunderstand her meaning, exclaimed reproachfully, "I was not thinking of myself. In the time to come, whatever be my lot, I shall have the one consolation, that this is best for you. Think of your mother."

"She will love you," Gavin said, "when I tell her of you."

"Yes," said Babbie, wringing her hands; "she will almost love me, but for what? For not marrying you. That is the only reason any one in Thrums will have for wishing me well."

"No others," Gavin answered, "will ever know why I remained unmarried."

"Will you never marry?" Babbie asked, exultingly. "Ah!" she cried, ashamed, "but you must."

"Never."

Well, many a man and many a woman has made that vow in similar circumstances, and not all have kept it. But shall we who are old smile cynically at the brief and burning passion of the young? "The day," you say, "will come when —— " Good sir, hold your peace. Their agony was great, and now is dead, and, maybe, they have forgotten where it lies buried; but dare you answer lightly when I ask you which of these things is saddest?

Babbie believed his "Never," and, doubtless, thought no worse of him for it; but she saw no way of comforting him save by disparagement of herself.

"You must think of your congregation," she said. "A minister with a gypsy wife —— "

"Would have knocked them about with a flail," Gavin interposed, showing his teeth at the thought of the precentor, "until they did her reverence."

She shook her head, and told him of her meeting with Micah Dow. It silenced him; not, however, on account of its pathos, as she thought, but because it interpreted the riddle of Rob's behaviour.

"Nevertheless," he said ultimately, "my duty is not to do what is right in my people's eyes, but what seems right in my own."

Babbie had not heard him.

"I saw a face at the window just now," she whispered, drawing closer to him.

"There was no face there; the very thought of Rob Dow raises him before you," Gavin answered reassuringly, though Rob was nearer at that moment than either of them thought.

"I must go away at once," she said, still with her eyes on the window. "No, no, you shall not come or stay with me; it is you who are in danger."

"Do not fear for me."

"I must if you will not. Before you came in, did I not hear you speak of a meeting you had to attend to-night?"

"My pray —— " His teeth met on the word; so abruptly did it conjure up the forgotten prayer-meeting that before the shock could reach his mind he stood motionless, listening for the bell. For one instant all that had taken place since he last heard it might have happened between two of

its tinkles; Babbie passed from before him like a figure in a panorama, and he saw, instead, a congregation in their pews.

"What do you see?" Babbie cried in alarm, for he seemed to be gazing at the window.

"Only you," he replied, himself again; "I am coming with you."

"You must let me go alone," she entreated; "if not for your own safety" — but it was only him she considered — "then for the sake of Lord Rintoul. Were you and I to be seen together now, his name and mine might suffer."

It was an argument the minister could not answer, save by putting his hands over his face; his distress made Babbie strong; she moved to the door, trying to smile.

"Go, Babbie!" Gavin said, controlling his voice, though it had been a smile more pitiful than her tears. "God has you in His keeping; it is not His will to give me this to bear for you."

They were now in the garden.

"Do not think of me as unhappy," she said; "it will be happiness to me to try to be all you would have me be."

He ought to have corrected her. "All that God would have me be" is what she should have said. But he only replied, "You will be a good woman, and none such can be altogether unhappy; God sees to that."

He might have kissed her, and perhaps she thought so.

"I am — I am going now, dear," she said, and came back a step because he did not answer; then she went on, and was out of his sight at three yards' distance. Neither of them heard the approaching dog-cart.

"You see, I am bearing it quite cheerfully," she said. "I shall have everything a woman loves; do not grieve for me so much."

Gavin dared not speak nor move. Never had he found life so hard; but he was fighting with the ignoble in himself, and winning. She opened the gate, and it might have been a signal to the dog-cart to stop. They both heard a dog barking, and then the voice of Lord Rintoul —

"That is a light in the window. Jump down, McKenzie, and inquire."

Gavin took one step nearer Babbie, and stopped. He did not see how all her courage went from her, so that her knees yielded, and she held out her arms to him, but he heard a great sob and then his name.

"Gavin, I am afraid."

Gavin understood now, and I say he would have been no man to leave her after that; only a moment was allowed him, and it was their last chance on earth. He took it. His arm went round his beloved, and he drew her away from Nanny's.

372

THE APPALLING MARRIAGE

McKenzie found both house and garden empty. " And yet," he said, " I swear some one passed the window as we sighted it."

" Waste no more time," cried the impatient earl. " We must be very near the hill now. You will have to lead the horse, McKenzie, in this darkness ; the dog may find the way through the broom for us."

"The dog has run on," McKenzie replied, now in an evil temper. " Who knows, it may be with her now ? So we must feel our way cautiously ; there is no call for capsizing the trap in our haste." But there was call for haste if they were to reach the gypsy encampment before Gavin and Babbie were made man and wife over the tongs.

The Spittal dog-cart rocked as it dragged its way through the broom. Rob Dow followed. The ten o'clock bell began to ring.

CHAPTER XXXIII

WHILE THE TEN O'CLOCK BELL WAS RINGING

In the square and wynds — weavers in groups:

" No, no, Davit, Mr. Dishart hadna felt the blow the piper gave him till he ascended the pulpit to conduct the prayer-meeting for rain, and then he fainted awa. Tammas Whamond and Peter Tosh carried him to the Session-house. Ay, an awful scene."

" How did the minister no come to the meeting? I wonder how you could expect it, Snecky, and his mother taen so suddenly ill; he's at her bedside, but the doctor has little hope."

" This is what has occurred, Tailor: Mr. Dishart never got the length of the pulpit. He fell in a swound on the vestry floor. What caused it? Oh, nothing but the heat. Thrums is so dry that one spark would set it in a blaze."

" I canna get at the richts o' what kept him frae the meeting, Femie, but it had something to do wi' an Egyptian on the hill. Very like he had been trying to stop the gypsy marriage there. I

374

gaed to the manse to speir at Jean what was wrang, but I'm thinking I telled her mair than she could tell me."

" Man, man, Andrew, the wite o't lies wi' Peter Tosh. He thocht we was to hae sic a terrible rain that he implored the minister no to pray for it, and so angry was Mr. Dishart that he ordered the whole Session out o' the kirk. I saw them in Couthie's close, and michty dour they looked."

" Yes, as sure as death, Tammas Whamond locked the kirk-door in Mr. Dishart's face."

" I'm a' shaking? And small wonder, Marget, when I've heard this minute that Mr. Dishart's been struck by lichtning while looking for Rob Dow. He's no killed, but, woe's me! they say he'll never preach again."

" Nothing o' the kind. It was Rob that the lichtning struck dead in the doctor's machine. The horse wasna touched; it came tearing down the Roods wi' the corps sitting in the machine like a living man."

" What are you listening to, woman? Is it to a dog barking? I've heard it this while, but it's far awa."

In the manse kitchen :

" Jean, did you not hear me ring? I want you to —— Why are you staring out at the window, Jean?"

"I — I— was just hearkening to the ten o'clock bell, ma'am."

"I never saw you doing nothing before! Put the heater in the fire, Jean. I want to iron the minister's neckcloths. The prayer-meeting is long in coming out, is it not?"

"The — the drouth, ma'am, has been so cruel hard."

"And, to my shame, I am so comfortable that I almost forgot how others are suffering. But my son never forgets, Jean. You are not crying, are you?"

"No, ma'am."

"Bring the iron to the parlour, then. And if the minis—— Why did you start, Jean? I only heard a dog barking."

"I thocht, ma'am—at first I thocht it was Mr. Dishart opening the door. Ay, it's just a dog; some gypsy dog on the hill, I'm thinking, for sound would carry far the nicht."

"Even you, Jean, are nervous at nights, I see, if there is no man in the house. We shall hear no more distant dogs barking, I warrant, when the minister comes home."

"When he comes home, ma'am."

On the middle of the hill—a man and a woman:

"Courage, beloved; we are nearly there."

"But, Gavin, I cannot see the encampment."

"The night is too dark."

THE TEN O'CLOCK BELL

"But the gypsy fires?"

"They are in the Toad's-hole."

"Listen to that dog barking."

"There are several dogs at the encampment, Babbie."

"There is one behind us.   See, there it is!"

"I have driven it away, dear.   You are trembling."

"What we are doing frightens me, Gavin.   It is at your heels again!"

"It seems to know you."

"Oh, Gavin, it is Lord Rintoul's collie Snap. It will bite you."

"No, I have driven it back again.   Probably the earl is following us."

"Gavin, I cannot go on with this."

"Quicker, Babbie."

"Leave me, dear, and save yourself."

"Lean on me, Babbie."

"Oh, Gavin, is there no way but this?"

"No sure way."

"Even though we are married to-night——"

"We shall be married in five minutes, and then, whatever befall, he cannot have you."

"But after?"

"I will take you straight to the manse, to my mother."

"Were it not for that dog, I should think we were alone on the hill."

377

"But we are not. See, there are the gypsy fires."

On the west side of the hill — two figures:

"Tammas, Tammas Whamond, I've lost you. Should we gang to the manse down the fields?"

"Wheesht, Hendry!"

"What are you listening for?"

"I heard a dog barking."

"Only a gypsy dog, Tammas, barking at the coming storm."

"The gypsy dogs are all tied up, and this one's atween us and the Toad's-hole. What was that?"

"It was nothing but the rubbing of the branches in the cemetery on ane another. It's said, trees mak' that fearsome sound when they're terrified."

"It was a dog barking at somebody that's stoning it. I ken that sound, Hendry Munn."

"May I die the death, Tammas Whamond, if a great drap o' rain didna strike me the now, and I swear it was warm. I'm for running hame."

"I'm for seeing who drove awa that dog. Come back wi' me, Hendry."

"I winna. There's no a soul on the hill but you and me and thae daffing and drinking gypsies. How do you no answer me, Tammas? Hie, Tammas Whamond, whaur are you? He's gone! Ay, then I'll mak' tracks hame."

THE TEN O'CLOCK BELL

In the broom — a dog-cart:

" Do you see nothing yet, McKenzie ? "

"Scarce the broom at my knees, Rintoul. There is not a light on the hill."

"McKenzie, can that schoolmaster have deceived us ? "

" It is probable."

" Urge on the horse, however. There is a road through the broom, I know. Have we stuck again ? "

"Rintoul, she is not here. I promised to help you to bring her back to the Spittal before this escapade became known, but we have failed to find her. If she is to be saved now, it must be by herself. I daresay she has returned already. Let me turn the horse's head. There is a storm brewing."

" I will search this gypsy encampment first, if it is on the hill. Hark ! that was a dog's bark. Yes, it is Snap, but he would not bark at nothing. Why do you look behind you so often, McKenzie ? "

" For some time, Rintoul, it has seemed to me that we are being followed. Listen ! "

" I hear nothing. At last, McKenzie, at last, we are out of the broom."

" And as I live, Rintoul, I see the gypsy lights ! "

It might have been a lantern that was flashed across the hill. Then all that part of the world went suddenly on fire. Everything was horribly distinct in that white light. The firs of Caddam were so near that it seemed to have arrested them in a silent march upon the hill. The grass would not hide a pebble. The ground was scored with shadows of men and things. Twice the light flickered and recovered itself. A red serpent shot across it, and then again black night fell.

The hill had been illumined thus for nearly half a minute. During that time not even a dog stirred. The shadows of human beings lay on the ground as motionless as logs. What had been revealed seemed less a gypsy marriage than a picture. Or was it that during the ceremony every person on the hill had been turned into stone? The gypsy king, with his arm upraised, had not had time to let it fall. The men and women behind him had their mouths open, as if struck when on the point of calling out. Lord Rintoul had risen in the dog-cart, and was leaning forward. One of McKenzie's feet was on the shaft. The man crouching in the dog-cart's wake had flung up his hands to protect his face. The precentor, his neck outstretched, had a hand on each knee. All eyes were fixed, as in the death glare, on Gavin and Babbie, who stood before the king, their hands clasped over the tongs. Fear was petrified on the woman's face, determination on the man's.

They were all released by the crack of the thunder, but for another moment none could have swaggered.

" That was Lord Rintoul in the dog-cart," Babbie whispered, drawing in her breath.

" Yes, dear," Gavin answered, resolutely, " and now is the time for me to have my first and last talk with him. Remain here, Babbie. Do not move till I come back."

" But, Gavin, he has seen. I fear him still."

" He cannot touch you now, Babbie. You are my wife."

In the vivid light Gavin had thought the dog-cart much nearer than it was. He called Lord Rintoul's name, but got no answer. There were shouts behind, gypsies running from the coming rain, dogs whining, but silence in front. The minister moved on some paces. Away to the left he heard voices —

" Who was the man, McKenzie ? "

" My lord, I have lost sight of you. This is not the way to the camp."

" Tell me, McKenzie, that you did not see what I saw."

" Rintoul, I beseech you to turn back. We are too late."

" We are not too late."

Gavin broke through the darkness between them and him, but they were gone. He called to them, and stopped to listen to their feet.

"Is that you, Gavin?" Babbie asked just then.

For reply, the man who had crept up to her clapped his hand upon her mouth. Only the beginning of a scream escaped from her. A strong arm drove her quickly southward.

Gavin heard her cry, and ran back to the encampment. Babbie was gone. None of the gypsies had seen her since the darkness came back. He rushed hither and thither with a torch that only showed his distracted face to others. He flung up his arms in appeal for another moment of light; then he heard Babbie scream again, and this time it was from a distance. He dashed after her; he heard a trap speeding down the green sward through the broom.

Lord Rintoul had kidnapped Babbie. Gavin had no other thought as he ran after the dog-cart from which the cry had come. The earl's dog followed him, snapping at his heels. The rain began.

CHAPTER XXXIV

THE GREAT RAIN

GAVIN passed on through Windyghoul, thinking in his frenzy that he still heard the trap. In a rain that came down like iron rods every other sound was beaten dead. He slipped, and before he could regain his feet the dog bit him. To protect himself from dykes and trees and other horrors of the darkness he held his arm before him, but soon it was driven to his side. Wet whips cut his brow so, that he had to protect it with his hands, until it had to bear the lash again, for they would not. Now he was forced upon his knees, and would have succumbed, but for a dread of being pinned to the earth. This fight between the man and the rain went on all night, and, long before it ended, the man was past the power of thinking.

In the ringing of the ten o'clock bell Gavin had lived the seventh part of a man's natural life. Only action was required of him. That accomplished, his mind had begun to work again, when suddenly the loss of Babbie stopped it, as we may put out a fire with a great coal. The last thing he had reflected about was a dog-cart in motion, and, consequently, this idea clung to him. His church, his mother, were lost knowledge of, but still he seemed to hear the trap in front.

The rain increased in violence, appalling even those who heard it from under cover. However rain may storm, though it be an army of archers battering roofs and windows, it is only terrifying when the noise swells every instant. In those hours of darkness it again and again grew in force and doubled its fury, and was louder, louder, and louder, until its next attack was to be more than men and women could listen to. They held each other's hands and stood waiting. Then abruptly it abated, and people could speak. I believe a rain that became heavier every second for ten minutes would drive many listeners mad. Gavin was in it on a night that tried us repeatedly for quite half that time.

By-and-by even the vision of Babbie in the dog-cart was blotted out. If nothing had taken its place, he would not have gone on probably; and had he turned back objectless, his strength would have succumbed to the rain. Now he saw Babbie and Rintoul being married by a minister who was himself, and there was a fair company looking on, and always when he was on the point of shouting to himself, whom he could see clearly, that this woman was already married, the rain obscured his words and the light went out. Presently the ceremony began again, always to stop at the same point.   He saw it in the lightning-flash that had startled the hill.   It gave him courage to fight his way onward, because he thought he must be heard if he could draw nearer to the company.

A regiment of cavalry began to trouble him. He heard it advancing from the Spittal, but was not dismayed, for it was, as yet, far distant.   The horsemen came thundering on, filling the whole glen of Quharity.   Now he knew that they had been sent out to ride him down.   He paused in dread, until they had swept past him.   They came back to look for him, riding more furiously than ever, and always missed him, yet his fears of the next time were not lessened.   They were only the rain.

All through the night the dog followed him. He would forget it for a time, and then it would be so close that he could see it dimly.   He never heard it bark, but it snapped at him, and a gi͘ had become the expression of its face.   He sto͘ d it, he even flung himself at it, he addressed ͘ in caressing tones, and always with the resu͘ ͘hat it disappeared, to come back presently.

He found himself walking in a l͘ ͘, and now even the instinct of self-preservat͘ ͘ must have been flickering, for he waded or ͘ejoicing merely in getting rid of the dog.   Sor͘ ͘hing in the water rose and struck him.   Instea͘ ͘ stupefying him, the blow brought him to his ͘nses, and he struggled for his life.   The grour͘ ͘ slipped beneath his feet

many times, but at last he was out of the water.
That he was out in a flood he did not realise; yet
he now acted like one in full possession of his
faculties. When his feet sank in water, he drew
back; and many times he sought shelter behind
banks and rocks, first testing their firmness with
his hands. Once a torrent of stones, earth, and
heather carried him down a hill-side until he struck
against a tree. He twined his arms round it, and
had just done so when it fell with him. After that,
when he touched trees growing in water, he fled from
them, thus probably saving himself from death.

What he heard now might have been the roll
and crack of the thunder. It sounded in his ear
like nothing else. But it was really something
that swept down the hill in roaring spouts of water,
and it passed on both sides of him so, that at one
moment, had he paused, it would have crashed into
him, and at another he was only saved by stopping. He felt that the struggle in the dark was to
go on till the crack of doom.

Then he cast himself upon the ground. It moved
beneath him like some great animal, and he rose
and stole away from it. Several times did this
happen. The stones against which his feet struck
seemed to acquire life from his touch. So strong
had he become, or so weak all other things, that
whatever clump he laid hands on by which to pull
himself out of the water was at once rooted up.

THE GREAT RAIN

The daylight would not come. He longed passionately for it. He tried to remember what it was like, and could not; he had been blind so long. It was away in front somewhere, and he was struggling to overtake it. He expected to see it from a dark place, when he would rush forward to bathe his arms in it, and then the elements that were searching the world for him would see him and he would perish. But death did not seem too great a penalty to pay for light.

And at last day did come back, grey and drear. He saw suddenly once more. I think he must have been wandering the glen with his eyes shut, as one does shut them involuntarily against the hidden dangers of black night. How different was daylight from what he had expected! He looked, and then shut his dazed eyes again, for the darkness was less horrible than the day. Had he indeed seen, or only dreamed that he saw? Once more he looked to see what the world was like; and the sight that met his eyes was so mournful that he who had fought through the long night now sank hopeless and helpless among the heather. The dog was not far away, and it, too, lost heart. Gavin held out his hand, and Snap crept timidly toward him. He unloosened his coat, and the dog nestled against him, cowed and shivering, hiding its head from the day. Thus they lay, and the rain beat upon them.

CHAPTER XXXV

THE GLEN AT BREAK OF DAY

MY first intimation that the burns were in flood came from Waster Lunny, close on the strike of ten o'clock. This was some minutes before they had any rain in Thrums. I was in the school-house, now piecing together the puzzle Lord Rintoul had left with me, and anon starting upright as McKenzie's hand seemed to tighten on my arm. Waster Lunny had been whistling to me (with his fingers in his mouth) for some time before I heard him and hurried out. I was surprised and pleased, knowing no better, to be met on the threshold by a whisk of rain.

The night was not then so dark but that when I reached the Quharity I could see the farmer take shape on the other side of it. He wanted me to exult with him, I thought, in the end of the drought, and I shouted that I would fling him the stilts.

"It's yoursel' that wants them," he answered, excitedly, "if you're fleid to be left alone in the school-house the nicht. Do you hear me, do-

388

minie? There has been frichtsome rain among
the hills, and the Bog burn is coming down like a
sea. It has carried awa the miller's brig, and the
steading o' Muckle Pirley is standing three feet in
water."

"You're dreaming, man," I roared back, but
beside his news he held my doubts of no account.

"The Retery's in flood," he went on, "and running wild through Hazel Wood; T'nowdunnie's
tattie field's out o' sicht, and at the Kirkton they're
fleid they've lost twa kye."

"There has been no rain here," I stammered,
incredulously.

"It's coming now," he replied. "And listen;
the story's out that the Backbone has fallen into
the loch. You had better cross, dominie, and
thole out the nicht wi' us."

The Backbone was a piece of mountain-side
overhanging a loch among the hills, and legend
said that it would one day fall forward and squirt
all the water into the glen. Something of the
kind had happened, but I did not believe it then;
with little wit I pointed to the shallow Quharity.

"It may come down at any minute," the farmer
answered, "and syne, mind you, you'll be five
miles frae Waster Lunny, for there'll be no crossing but by the Brig o' March. If you winna come,
I maun awa back. I mauna bide langer on the
wrang side o' the Moss ditch, though it has been

as dry this month back as a rabbit's roady. But if you——" His voice changed. "God's sake, man," he cried, "you're ower late. Look at that! Dinna look—run, run!"

If I had not run before he bade me, I might never have run again on earth. I had seen a great shadowy yellow river come riding down the Quharity. I sprang from it for my life: and when next I looked behind, it was upon a turbulent loch, the further bank lost in darkness. I was about to shout to Waster Lunny, when a monster rose in the torrent between me and the spot where he had stood. It frightened me to silence until it fell, when I knew it was but a tree that had been flung on end by the flood. For a time there was no answer to my cries, and I thought the farmer had been swept away. Then I heard his whistle, and back I ran recklessly through the thickening darkness to the school-house. When I saw the tree rise, I had been on ground hardly wet as yet with the rain; but by the time Waster Lunny sent that reassuring whistle to me I was ankle-deep in water, and the rain was coming down like hail. I saw no lightning.

For the rest of the night I was only out once, when I succeeded in reaching the hen-house, and brought all my fowls safely to the kitchen, except a hen which would not rise off her young. Between us we had the kitchen floor, a pool of water;

and the rain had put out my fires already, as ef-
fectually as if it had been an overturned broth-pot.
That I never took off my clothes that night I need
not say, though of what was happening in the glen
I could only guess.   A flutter against my window
now and again, when the rain had abated, told me
of another bird that had flown there to die; and
with Waster Lunny I kept up communication by
waving a light, to which he replied in a similar
manner.   Before morning, however, he ceased to
answer my signals, and I feared some catastrophe
had occurred at the farm.   As it turned out, the
family was fighting with the flood for the year's
shearing of wool, half of which eventually went
down the waters, with the wool-shed on top of it.

The school-house stands too high to fear any
flood, but there were moments when I thought
the rain would master it.   Not only the windows
and the roof were rattling then, but all the walls,
and I was like one in a great drum.   When the
rain was doing its utmost, I heard no other sound;
but when the lull came, there was the wash of a
heavy river, or a crack as of artillery that told
of landslips, or the plaintive cry of the peesweep
as it rose in the air, trying to entice the waters
away from its nest.

It was a dreary scene that met my gaze at break
of day.   Already the Quharity had risen six feet,
and in many parts of the glen it was two hundred

391

yards wide. Waster Lunny's corn-field looked
like a bog grown over with rushes, and what had
been his turnips had become a lake with small
islands in it. No dyke stood whole except one
that the farmer, unaided, had built in a straight
line from the road to the top of Mount Bare, and
my own, the further end of which dipped in water.
Of the plot of firs planted fifty years earlier to
help on Waster Lunny's crops, only a triangle had
withstood the night.

Even with the aid of my field-glass I could not
estimate the damage on more distant farms, for
the rain, though now thin and soft, as it continued
for six days, was still heavy and of a brown colour.
After breakfast—which was interrupted by my
bantam cock's twice spilling my milk—I saw
Waster Lunny and his son, Matthew, running
towards the shepherd's house with ropes in their
hands. The house, I thought, must be in the mist
beyond; and then I sickened, knowing all at once
that it should be on this side of the mist. When
I had nerve to look again, I saw that though the
roof had fallen in, the shepherd was astride one of
the walls, from which he was dragged presently
through the water by the help of the ropes. I remember noticing that he returned to his house
with the rope still about him, and concluding that
he had gone back to save some of his furniture.
I was wrong, however. There was too much to

be done at the farm to allow this, but Waster
Lunny had consented to Duncan's forcing his way
back to the shieling to stop the clock. To both
men it seemed horrible to let a clock go on ticking
in a deserted house.

Having seen this rescue accomplished, I was
letting my glass roam in the opposite direction,
when one of its shakes brought into view something on my own side of the river. I looked at
it long, and saw it move slightly. Was it a human being? No, it was a dog. No, it was a
dog and something else. I hurried out to see
more clearly, and after a first glance the glass
shook so in my hands that I had to rest it on the
dyke. For a full minute, I daresay, did I look
through the glass without blinking, and then I
needed to look no more. That black patch was,
indeed, Gavin.

He lay quite near the school-house, but I had to
make a circuit of half a mile to reach him. It
was pitiful to see the dog doing its best to come
to me, and falling every few steps. The poor brute
was discoloured almost beyond recognition; and
when at last it reached me, it lay down at my feet
and licked them. I stepped over it and ran on
recklessly to Gavin. At first I thought he was
dead. If tears rolled down my cheeks, they were
not for him.

I was no strong man even in those days, but I

carried him to the school-house, the dog crawling
after us. Gavin I put upon my bed, and I lay down
beside him, holding him close to me, that some of
the heat of my body might be taken in by his.
When he was able to look at me, however, it was
not with understanding, and in vain did my anxiety press him with questions. Only now and
again would some word in my speech strike upon
his brain and produce at least an echo. To " Did
you meet Lord Rintoul's dog-cart ? " he sat up,
saying quickly —

" Listen, the dog-cart ! "

" Egyptian " was not that forenoon among the
words he knew, and I did not think of mentioning
" hill." At " rain " he shivered ; but " Spittal "
was what told me most.

" He has taken her back," he replied at once,
from which I learned that Gavin now knew as
much of Babbie as I did.

I made him as comfortable as possible, and de-
spairing of learning anything from him in his present state, I let him sleep. Then I went out into
the rain, very anxious, and dreading what he might
have to tell me when he woke. I waded and
jumped my way as near to the farm as I dared go,
and Waster Lunny, seeing me, came to the water's
edge. At this part the breadth of the flood was
not forty yards, yet for a time our voices could no

more cross its roar than one may send a snowball through a stone wall. I know not whether the river then quieted for a space, or if it was only that the ears grow used to dins as the eyes distinguish the objects in a room that is at first black to them, but after a little we were able to shout our remarks across, much as boys fling pebbles, many to fall into the water, but one occasionally to reach the other side. Waster Lunny would have talked of the flood, but I had not come here for that.

"How were you home so early from the prayer-meeting last night?" I bawled.

"No meeting . . . . I came straucht hame . . . . but terrible stories . . . . Mr. Dishart," was all I caught after Waster Lunny had flung his words across a dozen times.

I could not decide whether it would be wise to tell him that Gavin was in the school-house, and while I hesitated he continued to shout —

"Some woman . . . . the Session . . . . Lang Tammas . . . . God forbid . . . . maun back to the farm . . . byre running like a mill-dam."

He signed to me that he must be off, but my signals delayed him, and after much trouble he got my question, "Any news about Lord Rintoul?" My curiosity about the earl must have surprised him, but he answered —

"Marriage is to be the day . . . . cannon."

I signed that I did not grasp his meaning.

" A cannon is to be fired as soon as they're man and wife," he bellowed. " We'll hear it."

With that we parted. On my way home, I remember, I stepped on a brood of drowned partridge. I was only out half an hour, but I had to wring my clothes as if they were fresh from the tub.

The day wore on, and I did not disturb the sleeper. A dozen times, I suppose, I had to relight my fire of wet peats and roots; but I had plenty of time to stare out at the window, plenty of time to think. Probably Gavin's life depended on his sleeping, but that was not what kept my hands off him. Knowing so little of what had happened in Thrums since I left it, I was forced to guess, and my conclusion was that the earl had gone off with his own, and that Gavin in a frenzy had followed them. My wisest course, I thought, was to let him sleep until I heard the cannon, when his struggle for a wife must end. Fifty times at least did I stand regarding him as he slept; and if I did not pity his plight sufficiently, you know the reason. What were Margaret's sufferings at this moment? Was she wringing her hands for her son lost in the flood, her son in disgrace with the congregation? By one o'clock no cannon had sounded, and my suspense had become intolerable. I shook Gavin awake, and even as I shook him demanded a knowledge of all that had happened since we parted at Nanny's gate.

"How long ago is that?" he asked, with bewilderment.

"It was last night," I answered. "This morning I found you senseless on the hillside, and brought you here, to the Glen Quharity schoolhouse. That dog was with you."

He looked at the dog, but I kept my eyes on him, and I saw intelligence creep back, like a blush, into his face.

"Now I remember," he said, shuddering. "You have proved yourself my friend, sir, twice in the four-and-twenty hours."

"Only once, I fear," I replied gloomily. "I was no friend when I sent you to the earl's bride last night."

"You know who she is?" he cried, clutching me, and finding it agony to move his limbs.

"I know now," I said, and had to tell him how I knew before he would answer another question. Then I became listener, and you who read know to what alarming story.

"And all that time," I cried reproachfully, when he had done, "you gave your mother not a thought."

"Not a thought," he answered, and I saw that he pronounced a harsher sentence on himself than could have come from me. "All that time!" he repeated, after a moment. "It was only a few minutes, while the ten o'clock bell was ringing."

"Only a few minutes," I said, "but they changed the channel of the Quharity, and perhaps they have done not less to you."

"That may be," he answered gravely, "but it is of the present I must think just now. Mr. Ogilvy, what assurance have I, while lying here helpless, that the marriage at the Spittal is not going on?"

"None, I hope," I said to myself, and listened longingly for the cannon. But to him I only pointed out that no woman need go through a form of marriage against her will.

"Rintoul carried her off with no possible purport," he said, "but to set my marriage at defiance, and she has had a conviction always that to marry me would be to ruin me. It was only in the shiver Lord Rintoul's voice in the darkness sent through her that she yielded to my wishes. If she thought that marriage last night could be annulled by another to-day, she would consent to the second, I believe, to save me from the effects of the first. You are incredulous, sir; but you do not know of what sacrifices love is capable."

Something of that I knew, but I did not tell him. I had seen from his manner rather than his words that he doubted the validity of the gypsy marriage, which the king had only consented to celebrate because Babbie was herself an Egyptian. The ceremony had been interrupted in the middle.

" It was no marriage," I said, with a confidence I was far from feeling.

" In the sight of God," he replied excitedly, " we took each other for man and wife."

I had to hold him down in bed.

" You are too weak to stand, man," I said, " and yet you think you could start off this minute for the Spittal."

" I must go," he cried. " She is my wife. That impious marriage may have taken place already."

" Oh that it had!" was my prayer. " It has not," I said to him. " A cannon is to be fired immediately after the ceremony, and all the glen will hear it."

I spoke on the impulse, thinking to allay his desire to be off; but he said, " Then I may yet be in time." Somewhat cruelly I let him rise, that he might realise his weakness. Every bone in him cried out at his first step, and he sank into a chair.

" You will go to the Spittal for me?" he implored.

" I will not," I told him. " You are asking me to fling away my life."

To prove my words I opened the door, and he saw what the flood was doing. Nevertheless, he rose and tottered several times across the room, trying to revive his strength. Though every bit of him was aching, I saw that he would make the attempt.

"Listen to me," I said. "Lord Rintoul can maintain with some reason that it was you rather than he who abducted Babbie. Nevertheless, there will not, I am convinced, be any marriage at the Spittal to-day. When he carried her off from the Toad's-hole, he acted under impulses not dissimilar to those that took you to it. Then, I doubt not, he thought possession was all the law, but that scene on the hill has staggered him by this morning. Even though she thinks to save you by marrying him, he will defer his wedding until he learns the import of yours."

I did not believe in my own reasoning, but I would have said anything to detain him until that cannon was fired. He seemed to read my purpose, for he pushed my arguments from him with his hands, and continued to walk painfully to and fro.

"To defer the wedding," he said, "would be to tell all his friends of her gypsy origin, and of me. He would risk much to avoid that."

"In any case," I answered, "you must now give some thought to those you have forgotten, your mother and your church."

"That must come afterwards," he said firmly. "My first duty is to my wife."

The door swung-to sharply just then, and he started. He thought it was the cannon.

"I wish to God it had been!" I cried, interpreting his thoughts.

"Why do you wish me ill?" he asked.

"Mr. Dishart," I said solemnly, rising and facing him, and disregarding his question, "if that woman is to be your wife, it will be at a cost you cannot estimate till you return to Thrums. Do you think that if your congregation knew of this gypsy marriage they would have you for their minister for another day? Do you enjoy the prospect of taking one who might be an earl's wife into poverty — ay, and disgraceful poverty? Do you know your mother so little as to think she could survive your shame? Let me warn you, sir, of what I see. I see another minister in the Auld Licht kirk; I see you and your wife stoned through our wynds, stoned from Thrums, as malefactors have been chased out of it ere now; and as certainly as I see these things I see a hearse standing at the manse door, and stern men denying a son's right to help to carry his mother's coffin to it. Go your way, sir, but first count the cost."

His face quivered before these blows, but all he said was, "I must dree my dreed."

"God is merciful," I went on, "and these things need not be. He is more merciful to you, sir, than to some, for the storm that He sent to

401

save you is ruining them. And yet the farmers are to-day thanking Him for every pound of wool, every blade of corn He has left them, while you turn from Him because He would save you, not in your way, but in His. It was His hand that stayed your marriage. He meant Babbie for the earl; and if it is on her part a loveless match, she only suffers for her own sins. Of that scene on the hill no one in Thrums, or in the glen, need ever know. Rintoul will see to it that the gypsies vanish from these parts for ever, and you may be sure the Spittal will soon be shut up. He and Mc-Kenzie have as much reason as yourself to be silent. You, sir, must go back to your congregation, who have heard as yet only vague rumours that your presence will dispel. Even your mother will remain ignorant of what has happened. Your absence from the prayer-meeting you can leave to me to explain."

He was so silent that I thought him mine, but his first words undeceived me.

"I thought I had nowhere so keen a friend," he said: "but, Mr. Ogilvy, it is devil's work you are pleading. Am I to return to my people to act a living lie before them to the end of my days? Do you really think that God devastated a glen to give me a chance of becoming a villain? No, sir, I am in His hands, and I will do what I think right."

"You will be dishonoured," I said, "in the sight of God and man."

"Not in God's sight," he replied. "It was a sinless marriage, Mr. Ogilvy, and I do not regret it. God ordained that she and I should love each other, and He put it into my power to save her from that man. I took her as my wife before Him, and in His eyes I am her husband. Knowing that, sir, how could I return to Thrums without her?"

I had no answer ready for him. I knew that in my grief for Margaret I had been advocating an unworthy course; but I would not say so. I went gloomily to the door, and there, presently, his hand fell on my shoulder.

"Your advice came too late, at any rate," he said. "You forget that the precentor was on the hill and saw everything."

It was he who had forgotten to tell me this, and to me it was the most direful news of all.

"My God!" I cried. "He will have gone to your mother and told her." And straightway I began to lace my boots.

"Where are you going?" he asked, staring at me.

"To Thrums," I answered, harshly.

"You said that to venture out into the glen was to court death," he reminded me.

"What of that?" I said, and hastily put on my coat.

"Mr. Ogilvy," he cried, "I will not allow you to do this for me."

"For you?" I said bitterly. "It is not for you."

I would have gone at once, but he got in front of me, asking, "Did you ever know my mother?"

"Long ago," I answered shortly, and he said no more; thinking, I suppose, that he knew all. He limped to the door with me, and I had only advanced a few steps when I understood better than before what were the dangers I was to venture into. Since I spoke to Waster Lunny the river had risen several feet, and even the hillocks in his turnip-field were now submerged. The mist was creeping down the hills. But what warned me most sharply that the flood was not satisfied yet was the top of the school-house dyke; it was lined with field-mice. I turned back, and Gavin, mistaking my meaning, said I did wisely.

"I have not changed my mind," I told him, and then had some difficulty in continuing. "I expect," I said, "to reach Thrums safely, even though I should be caught in the mist, but I shall have to go round by the Kelpie brig in order to get across the river, and it is possible that — that something may befall me."

I have all my life been something of a coward, and my voice shook when I said this, so that Gavin again entreated me to remain at the school-house, saying that if I did not he would accompany me.

"And so increase my danger tenfold," I pointed out. "No, no, Mr. Dishart, I go alone; and if I can do nothing with the congregation, I can at least send your mother word that you still live. But if anything should happen to me, I want you ——"

But I could not say what I had come back to say. I had meant to ask him, in the event of my death, to take the hundred pounds which were the savings of my life; but now I saw that this might lead to Margaret's hearing of me, and so I stayed my words. It was bitter to me this, and yet, after all, a little thing when put aside the rest.

"Good-bye, Mr. Dishart," I said abruptly. I then looked at my desk, which contained some trifles that were once Margaret's. "Should anything happen to me," I said, "I want that old desk to be destroyed unopened."

"Mr. Ogilvy," he answered gently, "you are venturing this because you loved my mother. If anything does befall you, be assured that I will tell her what you attempted for her sake."

I believe he thought it was to make some such request that I had turned back.

"You must tell her nothing about me," I exclaimed in consternation. "Swear that my name will never cross your lips before her. No, that is not enough. You must forget me utterly, whether I live or die, lest sometime you should think of me and she should read your thoughts. Swear, man."

"Must this be?" he said, gazing at me.

"Yes," I answered more calmly, "it must be. For nearly a score of years I have been blotted out of your mother's life, and since she came to Thrums my one care has been to keep my existence from her. I have changed my burying-ground even from Thrums to the glen, lest I should die before her, and she, seeing the hearse go by the Tenements, might ask, 'Whose funeral is this?'"

In my anxiety to warn him, I had said too much. His face grew haggard, and there was fear to speak on it; and I saw, I knew, that some damnable suspicion of Margaret ——

"She was my wife!" I cried sharply. "We were married by the minister of Harvie. You are my son."

CHAPTER XXXVI

STORY OF THE DOMINIE

WHEN I spoke next, I was back in the school-house, sitting there with my bonnet on my head, Gavin looking at me. We had forgotten the cannon at last.

In that chair I had anticipated this scene more than once of late. I had seen that a time might come when Gavin would have to be told all, and I had even said the words aloud, as if he were indeed opposite me. So now I was only repeating the tale, and I could tell it without emotion, because it was nigh nineteen years old; and I did not look at Gavin, for I knew that his manner of taking it could bring no change to me.

".Did you never ask your mother," I said, addressing the fire rather than him, "why you were called Gavin?"

"Yes," he answered, "it was because she thought Gavin a prettier name than Adam."

"No," I said slowly, "it was because Gavin is my name. You were called after your father. Do you not remember my taking you one day to the shore at Harvie to see the fishermen carried to their boats upon their wives' backs, that they might start dry on their journey?"

"No," he had to reply. "I remember the women carrying the men through the water to the boats, but I thought it was my father who — I mean ——"

"I know whom you mean," I said. "That was our last day together, but you were not three years old. Yet you remembered me when you came to Thrums. You shake your head, but it is true. Between the diets of worship that first Sabbath I was introduced to you, and you must have had some shadowy recollection of my face, for you asked, 'Surely I saw you in church in the forenoon, Mr. Ogilvy?' I said 'Yes,' but I had not been in the church in the forenoon. You have forgotten even that, and yet I treasured it."

I could hear that he was growing impatient, though so far he had been more indulgent than I had any right to expect.

"It can all be put into a sentence," I said calmly. "Margaret married Adam Dishart, and afterwards, believing herself a widow, she married me. You were born, and then Adam Dishart came back."

That is my whole story, and here was I telling it to my son, and not a tear between us. It ended abruptly, and I fell to mending the fire.

"When I knew your mother first," I went on,

after Gavin had said some boyish things that were
of no avail to me, "I did not think to end my
days as a dominie. I was a student at Aberdeen,
with the ministry in my eye, and sometimes on
Saturdays I walked forty miles to Harvie to go to
church with her. She had another lover, Adam
Dishart, a sailor turned fisherman; and while I
lingered at corners, wondering if I could dare to
meet her and her mother on their way to church,
he would walk past with them. He was accom-
panied always by a lanky black dog, which he
had brought from a foreign country. He never
signed for any ship without first getting permission
to take it with him, and in Harvie they said it did
not know the language of the native dogs. I have
never known a man and dog so attached to each
other."

"I remember that black dog," Gavin said. "I
have spoken of it to my mother, and she shuddered, as if it had once bitten her."

"While Adam strutted by with them," I continued, "I would hang back, raging at his assurance or my own timidity; but I lost my next
chance in the same way. In Margaret's presence
something came over me, a kind of dryness in the
throat, that made me dumb. I have known divin-
ity students stricken in the same way, just as they
were giving out their first text. It is no aid in
getting a kirk or wooing a woman.

"If anyone in Harvie recalls me now, it is as a hobbledehoy who strode along the cliffs, shouting Homer at the sea-mews. With all my learning, I, who gave Margaret the name of Lalage, understood women less than any fisherman who bandied words with them across a boat. I remember a Yule night when both Adam and I were at her mother's cottage, and, as we were leaving, he had the audacity to kiss Margaret. She ran out of the room, and Adam swaggered off, and, when I recovered from my horror, I apologised for what he had done. I shall never forget how her mother looked at me, and said, 'Ay, Gavin, I see they dinna teach everything at Aberdeen.' You will not believe it, but I walked away doubting her meaning. I thought more of scholarship then than I do now. Adam Dishart taught me its proper place.

"Well, that is the dull man I was; and yet, though Adam was always saying and doing the things I was making up my mind to say and do, I think Margaret cared more for me. Nevertheless, there was something about him that all women seemed to find lovable, a dash that made them send him away and then well-nigh run after him. At any rate, I could have got her after her mother's death if I had been half a man. But I went back to Aberdeen to write a poem about her, and while I was at it Adam married her."

I opened my desk and took from it a yellow manuscript.

"Here," I said, " is the poem. You see, I never finished it."

I was fingering the thing grimly when Gavin's eye fell on something else in the desk. It was an ungainly clasp knife, as rusty as if it had spent a winter beneath a hedge.

"I seem to remember that knife," he said.

"Yes," I answered, "you should remember it. Well, after three months Adam tired of his wife."

I stopped again. This was a story in which only the pauses were eloquent.

"Perhaps I have no right to say he tired of her. One day, however, he sauntered away from Harvie whistling, his dog at his heels as ever, and was not seen again for nearly six years. When I heard of his disappearance I packed my books in that kist and went to Harvie, where I opened a school. You see, everyone but Margaret believed that Adam had fallen over the cliffs and been drowned."

"But the dog?" said Gavin.

"We were all sure that, if he had fallen over, it had jumped after him. The fisher-folk said that he could have left his shadow behind as easily as it. Yet Margaret thought for long that he had tired of Harvie merely and gone back to sea, and not until two years had passed would she marry me. We lived in Adam's house. It was so near the little school that when I opened the window in summer-time she could hear the drone of our voices. During the weeks before you were born I kept that window open all day long, and often I went to it and waved my hand to her.

"Sometimes, when she was washing or baking, I brought you to the school. The only quarrel she and I ever had was about my teaching you the Lord's Prayer in Greek as soon as you could say father and mother. It was to be a surprise for her on your second birthday. On that day, while she was ironing, you took hold of her gown to steady yourself, and began 'Πάτερ ἡμῶν ὁ ἐν τοῖς οὐρανοῖς,' and to me, behind the door, it was music. But at ἁγιασθήτω, of which you made two syllables, you cried, and Margaret snatched you up, thinking this was some new ailment. After I had explained to her that it was the Lord's Prayer in Greek, she would let me take you to the school-house no more.

"Not much longer could I have taken you in any case, for already we are at the day when Adam Dishart came back. It was the 7th of September, and all the week most of the women in Harvie had been setting off at dawn to the harvest-fields and straggling home at nights, merry and with yellow corn in their hair. I had sat on in the school-house that day after my pupils were gone. I still meant to be a minister, and I was studying

Hebrew, and so absorbed in my book that as the daylight went, I followed it step by step as far as my window, and there I read, without knowing, until I chanced to look up, that I had left my desk. I have not opened that book since.

" From the window I saw you on the waste ground that separated the school from our home. You were coming to me on your hands and feet, and stopping now and again to look back at your mother, who was at the door, laughing and shaking her fist at you. I beckoned to you, and took the book back to my desk to lock it up. While my head was inside the desk I heard the school-house door pushed open, and thinking it was you I smiled, without looking up. Then something touched my hand, and I still thought it was you; but I looked down, and I saw Adam Dishart's black dog.

" I did not move. It looked up at me and wagged its tail. Then it drew back; I suppose, because I had no words for it. I watched it run half round the room, and stop and look at me again. Then it slunk out.

" All that time one of my hands had been holding the desk open. Now the lid fell. I put on my bonnet and went to the door. You were only a few yards away, with flowers in your fist. Margaret was laughing still. I walked round the school, and there was no dog visible. Margaret nodded to me, meaning that I should bring you

413

home. You thrust the flowers into my hand, but they fell. I stood there, dazed.

"I think I walked with you some way across the waste ground. Then I dropped your hand, and strode back to the school. I went down on my knees, looking for marks of a dog's paws, and I found them.

"When I came out again, your mother was no longer at our door, and you were crying because I had left you. I passed you and walked straight to the house. Margaret was skinning rushes for wicks. There must have been fear in my face, for as soon as she saw it she ran to the door to see if you were still alive. She brought you in with her, and so had strength to cry, 'What is it? Speak!'

"'Come away,' I said, 'come away,' and I was for drawing her to the door, but she pressed me into a chair. I was up again at once.

"'Margaret,' I said, 'ask no questions. Put on your bonnet, give me the boy, and let us away.'

"I could not take my eyes off the door, and she was walking to it to look out when I barred the way with my arm.

"'What have you seen?' she cried; and then, as I only pointed to her bonnet, she turned to you, and you said, 'Was it the black dog, father?'

"Gavin, then she knew; and I stood helpless and watched my wife grow old. In that moment she lost the sprightliness I loved the more, because I had none of it myself, and the bloom went from her face, never to return.

" 'He has come back,' she said.

" I told her what I had seen, and while I spoke she put on her bonnet, and I exulted, thinking — and then she took off her bonnet, and I knew she would not go away with me.

" 'Margaret,' I cried, 'I am that bairn's father.'

" 'Adam's my man,' she said, and at that I gave her a look for which God might have struck me dead. But instead of blaming me she put her arms round my neck.

"After that we said very little. We sat at opposite sides of the fire, waiting for him, and you played on the floor. The harvesters trooped by, and there was a fiddle; and when it stopped, long stillness, and then a step. It was not Adam. You fell asleep, and we could hear nothing but the sea. There was a harvest moon.

"Once a dog ran past the door, and we both rose. Margaret pressed her hands on her breast. Sometimes she looked furtively at me, and I knew her thoughts. To me it was only misery that had come, but to her it was shame, so that when you woke and climbed into her lap she shivered at your touch. I could not look at her after that, for there was a horror of me growing in her face.

"Ten o'clock struck, and then again there was

415

no sound but the sea pouring itself out on the beach. It was long after this, when to me there was still no other sound, that Margaret screamed, and you hid behind her. Then I heard it.

" 'Gavin,' Margaret said to me, 'be a good man all your life.'

" It was louder now, and then it stopped. Above the wash of the sea we heard another sound — a sharp tap, tap. You said, 'I know what sound that is; it's a man knocking the ashes out of his pipe against his boot.'

" Then the dog pushed the door off the latch, and Adam lurched in. He was not drunk, but he brought the smell of drink into the room with him. He was grinning like one bringing rare news, and before she could shrink back or I could strike him he had Margaret in his arms.

" 'Lord, lass,' he said, with many jovial oaths, 'to think I'm back again! There, she's swounded. What folks be women, to be sure.'

" 'We thought you were dead, Adam,' she said, coming to.

" 'Bless your blue eyes,' he answered gleefully; 'often I says to myself, "Meggy will be thinking I'm with the fishes," and then I chuckles.'

" 'Where have you been all this time?' I demanded sternly.

" 'Gavin,' he said effusively, 'your hand. And don't look so feared, man; I bear no malice for what you've done. I heard all about it at the Cross Anchors.'

" ' Where have you been these five years and a half?' I repeated.

" ' Where have I no been, lad?' he replied.

" ' At Harvie,' I said.

" ' Right you are,' said he good-naturedly. 'Meggy, I had no intention of leaving you that day, though I was yawning myself to death in Harvie, but I sees a whaler, and I thinks, "That's a tidy boat and I'm a tidy man, and if they'll take me and the dog, off we go." '

" ' You never wrote to me,' Margaret said.

" ' I meant to send you some scrapes,' he answered, ' but it wasna till I changed ships that I had the chance, and then I minds, " Meggy kens I'm no hand with the pen." But I swear I often thought of you, lass; and look you here, that's better than letters, and so is that, and every penny of it is yours.'

" He flung two bags of gold upon the table, and their chink brought you out from behind your mother.

" ' Hallo!' Adam cried.

" ' He is mine,' I said. 'Gavin, come here.' But Margaret held you back.

" ' Here's a go,' Adam muttered, and scratched his head. Then be slapped his thigh. 'Gavin,' he said, in his friendliest way, ' we'll toss for him.'

"He pulled the knife that is now in my desk from his pocket, spat on it, and flung it up. 'Dry, the kid's ours, Meggy,' he explained; 'wet, he goes to Gavin.' I clenched my fist to —— But what was the use? He caught the knife, and showed it to me.

"'Dry,' he said triumphantly; 'so he is ours, Meggy. Kiddy, catch the knife. It is yours; and, mind, you have changed dads. And now that we have settled that, Gavin, there's my hand again.'

"I went away and left them, and I never saw Margaret again until the day you brought her to Thrums. But I saw you once, a few days after Adam came back. I was in the school-house, packing my books, and you were playing on the waste ground. I asked you how your mother was, and you said, 'She's fleid to come to the door till you gang awa, and my father's buying a boat.'

"'I'm your father,' I said; but you answered confidently —

"'You're no a living man. You're just a man I dreamed about; and I promised my mother no to dream about you again.'

"'I am your father,' I repeated.

"'My father's awa buying a fishing-boat,' you insisted; 'and when I speir at my mother whaur my first father is, she says I'm havering.'

"'Gavin Ogilvy is your name,' I said. 'No,'

you answered, ' I have a new name. My mother told me my name is aye to be Gavin Dishart now. She told me, too, to fling awa this knife my father gave me, and I've flung it awa a lot o' times, but I aye pick it up again.'

"'Give it to me,' I said, with the wicked thoughts of a fool in my head.

" That is how your knife came into my possession. I left Harvie that night in the carrier's cart. but I had not the heart to return to college. Accident brought me here, and I thought it a fitting place in which to bury myself from Margaret."

CHAPTER XXXVII

SECOND JOURNEY OF THE DOMINIE TO THRUMS DURING THE TWENTY-FOUR HOURS

HERE was a nauseous draught for me. Having finished my tale, I turned to Gavin for sympathy; and, behold, he had been listening for the cannon instead of to my final words. So, like an old woman at her hearth, we warm our hands at our sorrows and drop in faggots, and each thinks his own fire a sun, in presence of which all other fires should go out. I was soured to see Gavin prove this, and then I could have laughed without mirth, for had not my bitterness proved it too?

"And now," I said, rising, "whether Margaret is to hold up her head henceforth lies no longer with me, but with you."

It was not to that he replied.

"You have suffered long, Mr. Ogilvy," he said. "Father," he added, wringing my hand. I called him son; but it was only an exchange of musty words that we had found too late. A father is a poor estate to come into at two-and-twenty.

"I should have been told of this," he said.

420

" Your mother did right, sir," I answered slowly, but he shook his head.

" I think you have misjudged her," he said. " Doubtless while my fa——, while Adam Dishart lived, she could only think of you with pain, but after his death —— "

" After his death," I said quietly, " I was still so horrible to her that she left Harvie without letting a soul know whither she was bound. She dreaded my following her."

" Stranger to me," he said, after a pause, " than even your story is her being able to keep it from me. I believed no thought ever crossed her mind that she did not let me share."

" And none, I am sure, ever did," I answered, " save that, and such thoughts as a woman has with God only. It was my lot to bring disgrace on her. She thought it nothing less, and she has hidden it all these years for your sake, until now it is not burdensome. I suppose she feels that God has taken the weight off her. Now you are to put a heavier burden in its place."

He faced me boldly, and I admire him for it now.

" I cannot admit," he said, " that I did wrong in forgetting my mother for that fateful quarter of an hour. Babbie and I loved each other, and I was given the opportunity of making her mine or losing her for ever. Have you forgotten that all

this tragedy you have told me of only grew out of
your own indecision? I took the chance that you
let slip by."

"I had not forgotten it," I replied. "What else
made me tell you last night that Babbie was in
Nanny's house?"

"But now you are afraid — now when the deed
is done, when for me there can be no turning back.
Whatever be the issue, I should be a cur to return
to Thrums without my wife. Every minute I feel
my strength returning, and before you reach Thrums
I will have set out to the Spittal."

There was nothing to say after that. He came
with me in the rain as far as the dyke, warning me
against telling his people what was not true.

"My first part," I answered, "will be to send
word to your mother that you are in safety. After
that I must see Whamond. Much depends on
him."

"You will not go to my mother?"

"Not so long as she has a roof over her head,"
I said, "but that may not be for long."

So, I think, we parted — each soon to forget the
other in a woman.

But I had not gone far when I heard something
that stopped me as sharply as if it had been Mc-
Kenzie's hand once more on my shoulder. For a
second the noise appalled me, and then, before the
echo began, I knew it must be the Spittal cannon.

My only thought was one of thankfulness. Now Gavin must see the wisdom of my reasoning. I would wait for him until he was able to come with me to Thrums. I turned back, and in my haste I ran through water I had gone round before.

I was too late. He was gone, and into the rain. I shouted his name in vain; that he had started for the Spittal there could be no doubt, that he would ever reach it was less certain. The earl's collie was still crouching by the fire, and, thinking it might be a guide to him, I drove the brute to the door, and chased it in the direction he probably had taken. Not until it had run from me did I resume my own journey. I do not need to be told that you who read would follow Gavin now rather than me; but you must bear with the dominie for a little while yet, as I see no other way of making things clear.

In some ways I was not ill-equipped for my attempt. I do not know any one of our hillsides as it is known to the shepherd, to whom every rabbit-hole and glimmer of mica is a landmark; but he, like his flock, has only to cross a dyke to find himself in a strange land, while I have been everywhere in the glen.

In the foreground the rain slanted, transparent till it reached the ground, where a mist seemed to blow it along as wind ruffles grass. In the distance all was a driving mist. I have been out for per-

423

haps an hour in rains as wetting, and I have watched floods from my window, but never since have I known the fifth part of a season's rainfall in eighteen hours; and if there should be the like here again, we shall be found better prepared for it. Men have been lost in the glen in mists so thick that they could plunge their fingers out of sight in it as into a meal girnel; but this mist never came within twenty yards of me. I was surrounded by it, however, as if I was in a round tent; and out of this tent I could not walk, for it advanced with me. On the other side of this screen were horrible noises, at whose cause I could only guess, save now and again when a tongue of water was shot at my feet, or great stones came crashing through the canvas of mist. Then I ran wherever safety prompted, and thus tangled my bearings, until I was like that one in the child's game who is blindfolded and turned round three times that he may not know east from west.

Once I stumbled over a dead sheep and a living lamb; and in a clump of trees which puzzled me — for they were where I thought no trees should be — a wood-pigeon flew to me, but struck my breast with such force that I picked it up dead. I saw no other living thing, though half a dozen times I must have passed within cry of farmhouses. At one time I was in a corn-field, where I had to lift my hands to keep them out of water, and a dread filled me that I had wandered in a circle, and was still on Waster Lunny's land. I plucked some corn and held it to my eyes to see if it was green; but it was yellow, and so I knew that at last I was out of the glen.

People up here will complain if I do not tell how I found the farmer of Green Brae's fifty pounds. It is one of the best-remembered incidents of the flood, and happened shortly after I got out of the corn-field. A house rose suddenly before me, and I was hastening to it when as suddenly three of its walls fell. Before my mind could give a meaning to what my eyes told it, the water that had brought down the house had lifted me off my feet and flung me among waves. That would have been the last of the dominie had I not struck against a chest, then halfway on its voyage to the sea. I think the lid gave way under me; but that is surmise, for from the time the house fell till I was on the river in a kist that was like to be my coffin, is almost a blank. After what may have been but a short journey, though I had time in it to say my prayers twice, we stopped, jammed among fallen trees; and seeing a bank within reach, I tried to creep up it. In this there would have been little difficulty had not the contents of the kist caught in my feet and held on to them, like living things afraid of being left behind. I let down my hands to disentangle my feet, but failed; and then, grown desperate, I succeeded in reaching firm ground, dragging I knew not what after me. It proved to be a pillow-slip. Green Brae still shudders when I tell him that my first impulse was to leave the pillow-slip unopened. However, I ripped it up, for to undo the wet strings that had ravelled round my feet would have wearied even a man with a needle to pick open the knots; and among broken gimlets, the head of a grape, and other things no beggar would have stolen, I found a tin canister containing fifty pounds. Waster Lunny says that this should have made a religious man of Green Brae, and it did to this extent, that he called the fall of the cottar's house providential. Otherwise the cottar, at whose expense it may be said the money was found, remains the more religious man of the two.

At last I came to the Kelpie's Brig, and I could have wept in joy (and might have been better employed), when, like everything I saw on that journey, it broke suddenly through the mist, and seemed to run at me like a living monster. Next moment I ran back, for as I stepped upon the bridge I saw that I had been about to walk into the air. What was left of the Kelpie's Brig ended in mid-stream. Instead of thanking God for the light without which I should have gone abruptly to my death, I sat down, miserable and hopeless.

Presently I was up, and trudging to the Loups

of Malcolm. At the Loups the river runs narrow and deep between cliffs, and the spot is so called because one Malcolm jumped across it when pursued by wolves. Next day he returned boastfully to look at his jump, and gazing at it turned dizzy and fell into the river. Since that time chains have been hung across the Loups, to reduce the distance between the farms of Carwhimple and Keep-What-You-Can from a mile to a hundred yards. You must cross the chains on your breast. They were suspended there by Rob Angus, who was also the first to breast them.

But I never was a Rob Angus. When my pupils practise what they call the high jump, two small boys hold a string aloft, and the bigger ones run at it gallantly until they reach it, when they stop meekly and creep beneath. They will repeat this twenty times, and yet never, when they start for the string, seem to know where their courage will fail. Nay, they will even order the small boys to hold the string higher. I have smiled at this, but it was the same courage while the difficulty is far off that took me to the Loups. At sight of them I turned away.

I prayed to God for a little of the mettle of other men, and He heard me, for with my eyes shut I seemed to see Margaret beckoning from across the abyss as if she had need of me. Then I rose calmly and tested the chains, and crossed them on my breast. Many have done it with the same danger, at which they laugh, but without that vision I should have held back.

I was now across the river, and so had left the chance of drowning behind, but I was farther from Thrums than when I left the school-house, and this countryside was almost unknown to me. The mist had begun to clear, so that I no longer wandered into fields; but though I kept to the roads, I could not tell that they led toward Thrums, and in my exhaustion I had often to stand still. Then to make a new start in the mud was like pulling stakes out of the ground. So long as the rain faced me I thought I could not be straying far; but after an hour I lost this guide, for a wind rose that blew it in all directions.

In another hour, when I should have been drawing near Thrums, I found myself in a wood, and here I think my distress was greatest; nor is this to be marvelled at, for instead of being near Thrums, I was listening to the monotonous roar of the sea. I was too spent to reason, but I knew that I must have travelled direct east, and must be close to the German Ocean. I remember putting my back against a tree and shutting my eyes, and listening to the lash of the waves against the beach, and hearing the faint toll of a bell, and wondering listlessly on what lighthouse it was ringing. Doubtless I would have lain down to sleep for

ever had I not heard another sound near at hand.
It was the knock of a hammer on wood, and
might have been a fisherman mending his boat.
The instinct of self-preservation carried me to it,
and presently I was at a little house. A man was
standing in the rain, hammering new hinges to the
door; and though I did not recognise him, I saw
with bewilderment that the woman at his side was
Nanny.

"It's the dominie," she cried, and her brother
added —

"Losh, sir, you hinna the look o' a living man."

"Nanny," I said, in perplexity, "what are you
doing here?"

"Whaur else should I be?" she asked.

I pressed my hands over my eyes, crying,
"Where am I?"

Nanny shrank from me, but Sanders said,
"Has the rain driven you gyte man? You're in
Thrums."

"But the sea," I said, distrusting him. "I hear
it. Listen!"

"That's the wind in Windyghoul," Sanders answered, looking at me queerly. "Come awa into
the house."

CHAPTER XXXVIII

THRUMS DURING THE TWENTY-FOUR HOURS— DEFENCE OF THE MANSE

HARDLY had I crossed the threshold of the mud house when such a sickness came over me that I could not have looked up, though Nanny's voice had suddenly changed to Margaret's. Vaguely I knew that Nanny had put the kettle on the fire— a woman's first thought when there is illness in the house — and as I sat with my hands over my face I heard the water dripping from my clothes to the floor.

"Why is that bell ringing?" I asked at last, ignoring all questions and speaking through my fingers. An artist, I suppose, could paint all expression out of a human face. The sickness was having that effect on my voice.

"It's the Auld Licht bell," Sanders said; "and it's almost as fearsome to listen to as last nicht's rain. I wish I kent what they're ringing it for."

"Wish no sic things," said Nanny nervously. "There's things it's best to put off kenning as lang as we can."

"It's that ill-cleakit witch, Effie McBean, that

430

makes Nanny speak so doleful," Sanders told me.
" There was to be a prayer-meeting last nicht, but
Mr. Dishart never came to 't, though they rang
till they wraxed their arms; and now Effie says
it'll ring on by itsel' till he's brocht hame a corp.
The hellicat says the rain's a dispensation to drown
him in for neglect o' duty. Sal, I would think
little o' the Lord if He needed to create a new sea
to drown one man in. Nanny, you cuttie, that's
no swearing; I defy you to find a single lonely
oath in what I've said."

" Never mind Effie McBean," I interposed.
" What are the congregation saying about the
minister's absence ? "

" We ken little except what Effie told us,"
Nanny answered. " I was at Tilliedrum yestreen,
meeting Sanders as he got out o' the gaol, and that
awfu on-ding began when we was on the Bellies
Braes. We focht our way through it, but not a
soul did we meet; and wha would gang out the
day that can bide at hame ? Ay, but Effie says
it's kent in Thrums that Mr. Dishart has run off wi'
— wi' an Egyptian."

" You're waur than her, Nanny," Sanders said
roughly, " for you hae twa reasons for kenning
better. In the first place, has Mr. Dishart no
keeped you in siller a' the time I was awa ? and
for another, have I no been at the manse ? "

My head rose now.

"He gaed to the manse," Nanny explained, "to thank Mr. Dishart for being so good to me. Ay, but Jean wouldna let him in. I'm thinking that looks gey grey."

"Whatever was her reason," Sanders admitted, "Jean wouldna open the door; but I keeked in at the parlour window, and saw Mrs. Dishart in't looking very cosy-like and lauching; and do you think I would hae seen that if ill had come ower the minister?"

"Not if Margaret knew of it," I said to myself, and wondered at Whamond's forbearance.

"She had a skein o' worsted stretched out on her hands," Sanders continued, "and a young leddy was winding it. I didna see her richt, but she wasna a Thrums leddy."

"Effie McBean says she's his intended, come to call him to account," Nanny said; but I hardly listened, for I saw that I must hurry to Tammas Whamond's. Nanny followed me to the gate with her gown pulled over her head, and said excitedly—

"Oh, dominie, I warrant it's true. It'll be Babbie. Sanders doesna suspect, because I've telled him nothing about her. Oh, what's to be done? They were baith so good to me."

I could only tell her to keep what she knew to herself.

"Has Rob Dow come back?" I called out after I had started.

"Whaur frae?" she replied; and then I remembered that all these things had happened while Nanny was at Tilliedrum. In this life some of the seven ages are spread over two decades, and others pass as quickly as a stage play. Though a fifth of a season's rain had fallen in a night and a day, it had scarcely kept pace with Gavin.

I hurried to the town by the Roods. That brae was as deserted as the country roads, except where children had escaped from their mothers to wade in it. Here and there dams were keeping the water away from one door to send it with greater volume to another, and at points the ground had fallen in. But this I noticed without interest. I did not even realise that I was holding my head painfully to the side where it had been blown by the wind and glued by the rain. I have never held my head straight since that journey.

Only a few looms were going, their peddles in water. I was addressed from several doors and windows; once by Charles Yuill.

"Dinna pretend," he said, "that you've walked in frae the school-house alane. The rain chased me into this house yestreen, and here it has keeped me, though I bide no further awa than Tillyloss."

"Charles," I said in a low voice, "why is the Auld Licht bell ringing?"

"Hae you no heard about Mr. Dishart?" he asked. "Oh, man! that's Lang Tammas in the kirk by himsel', tearing at the bell to bring the folk thegither to depose the minister."

Instead of going to Whamond's house in the school wynd I hastened down the Banker's close to the kirk, and had almost to turn back, so choked was the close with floating refuse. I could see the bell swaying, but the kirk was locked, and I battered on the door to no purpose. Then, remembering that Hendry Munn lived in Coutt's trance, I set off for his house. He saw me crossing the square, but would not open his door until I was close to it.

"When I open," he cried, "squeeze through quick;" but though I did his bidding, a rush of water darted in before me. Hendry re-closed the door by flinging himself against it.

"When I saw you crossing the square," he said, "it was surprise enough to cure the hiccup."

"Hendry," I replied instantly, "why is the Auld Licht bell ringing?"

He put his finger to his lip. "I see," he said imperturbably, "you've met our folk in the glen and heard frae them about the minister."

"What folk?"

"Mair than half the congregation," he replied, "started for Glen Quharity twa hours syne to help the farmers. You didna see them?"

"No; they must have been on the other side of the river." Again that question forced my lips, "Why is the bell ringing?"

"Canny, dominie," he said, "till we're up the stair. Mysy Moncur's lug's at her key-hole listening to you."

"You lie, Hendry Munn," cried an invisible woman. The voice became more plaintive: "I ken a heap, Hendry, so you may as well tell me a'."

"Lick away at the bone you hae," the shoemaker replied heartlessly, and conducted me to his room up one of the few inside stairs then in Thrums. Hendry's oldest furniture was five boxes, fixed to the wall at such a height that children could climb into them from a high stool. In these his bairns slept, and so space was economised. I could never laugh at the arrangement, as I knew that Betty had planned it on her death-bed for her man's sake. Five little heads bobbed up in their beds as I entered, but more vexing to me was Wearyworld on a stool.

"In by, dominie," he said sociably. "Sal, you needna fear burning wi' a' that water on you. You're in mair danger o' coming a-boil."

"I want to speak to you alone, Hendry," I said bluntly.

"You winna put me out, Hendry?" the alarmed policeman entreated. "Mind, you said in sic weather you would be friendly to a brute beast. Ay, ay, dominie, what's your news? It's welcome, be it good or bad. You would meet the townsfolk in the glen, and they would tell you about Mr. Dishart. What, you hinna heard? Oh, sirs, he's a lost man. There would hae been a meeting the day to depose him if so many hadna gaen to the glen. But the morn'll do as weel. The very women is cursing him, and the laddies has begun to gather stanes. He's married on an Egyp——"

"Hendry!" I cried, like one giving an order.

"Wearyworld, step!" said Hendry sternly, and then added soft-heartedly, "Here's a bit news that'll open Mysy Moncur's door to you. You can tell her frae me that the bell's ringing just because I forgot to tie it up last nicht, and the wind's shaking it, and I winna gang out in the rain to stop it."

"Ay," the policeman said, looking at me sulkily, "she may open her door for that, but it'll no let me in. Tell me mair. Tell me wha the leddy at manse is."

"Out you go," answered Hendry. "Once she opens the door, you can shove your foot in, and syne she's in your power." He pushed Wearyworld out, and came back to me, saying, "It was best to tell him the truth, to keep him frae making up lies."

"But is it the truth? I was told Lang Tammas——"

"Ay, I ken that story; but Tammas has other work on hand."

"Then tie up the bell at once, Hendry," I urged.

"I canna," he answered gravely. "Tammas took the keys o' the kirk frae me yestreen, and winna gie them up. He says the bell's being rung by the hand o' God."

"Has he been at the manse? Does Mrs. Dishart know ——?"

"He's been at the manse twa or three times, but Jean barred him out. She'll let nobody in till the minister comes back, and so the mistress kens nothing. But what's the use o' keeping it frae her ony langer?"

"Every use," I said.

"None," answered Hendry sadly. "Dominie, the minister was married to the Egyptian on the hill last nicht, and Tammas was witness. Not only were they married, but they've ran aff thegither."

"You are wrong, Hendry," I assured him, telling as much as I dared. "I left Mr. Dishart in my house."

"What! But if that is so, how did he no come back wi' you?"

"Because he was nearly drowned in the flood."

"She'll be wi' him?"

"He was alone."

Hendry's face lit up dimly with joy, and then he shook his head. "Tammas was witness," he said. "Can you deny the marriage?"

437

"All I ask of you," I answered guardedly, "is to suspend judgment until the minister returns."

"There can be nothing done, at ony rate," he said, "till the folk themsel's come back frae the glen; and I needna tell you how glad we would a' be to be as fond o' him as ever. But Tammas was witness."

"Have pity on his mother, man."

"We've done the best for her we could," he replied. "We prigged wi' Tammas no to gang to the manse till he was sure the minister was living. 'For if he has been drowned,' we said, 'his mother need never ken what we were thinking o' doing.' Ay, and we are sorry for the young leddy, too."

"What young lady is this you all talk of?" I asked.

"She's his intended. Ay, you needna start. She has come a' the road frae Glasgow to challenge him about the gypsy. The pitiful thing is that Mrs. Dishart lauched awa her fears, and now they're baith waiting for his return, as happy as ignorance can make them."

"There is no such lady," I said.

"But there is," he answered, doggedly, "for she came in a machine late last nicht, and I was ane o' a dozen that baith heard and saw it through my window. It stopped at the manse near half an hour. What's mair, the lady hersel' was at

Sam'l Farquharson's in the Tenements the day for twa hours."

I listened in bewilderment and fear.

"Sam'l's bairn's down wi' scarlet fever and like to die, and him being a widow-man he has gone useless. You mauna blame the wives in the Tenements for hauding back. They're fleid to smit their ain litlins; and as it happens, Sam'l's friends is a' aff to the glen. Weel, he ran greeting to the manse for Mr. Dishart, and the lady heard him crying to Jean through the door, and what does she do but gang straucht to the Tenements wi' Sam'l. Her goodness has naturally put the folk on her side against the minister."

"This does not prove her his intended," I broke in.

"She was heard saying to Sam'l," answered the kirk-officer, "that the minister being awa, it was her duty to take his place. Yes, and though she little kent it, he was already married."

"Hendry," I said, rising, "I must see this lady at once. Is she still at Farquharson's house?"

"She may be back again by this time. Tammas set off for Sam'l's as soon as he heard she was there, but he just missed her. I left him there an hour syne. He was waiting for her, determined to tell her all."

I set off for the Tenements at once, declining Hendry's company. The wind had fallen, so that the bell no longer rang, but the rain was falling doggedly. The streets were still deserted. I pushed open the precentor's door in the school wynd, but there was no one in the house. Tibbie Birse saw me, and shouted from her door —

"Hae you heard o' Mr. Dishart? He'll never daur show face in Thrums again."

Without giving her a word I hastened to the Tenements.

"The leddy's no here," Sam'l Farquharson told me, "and Tammas is back at the manse again, trying to force his way in."

From Sam'l, too, I turned, with no more than a groan; but he cried after me, "Perdition on the man that has played that leddy false."

Had Margaret been at her window she must have seen me, so recklessly did I hurry up the minister's road, with nothing in me but a passion to take Whamond by the throat. He was not in the garden. The kitchen door was open. Jean was standing at it with her apron to her eyes.

"Tammas Whamond?" I demanded, and my face completed the question.

"You're ower late," she wailed. "He's wi' her. Oh, dominie, whaur's the minister?"

"You base woman!" I cried, "why did you unbar the door?"

"It was the mistress," she answered. "She heard him shaking it, and I had to tell her wha it was. Dominie, it's a' my wite! He tried to get in last nicht, and roared threats through the door, and after he had gone awa she speired wha I had been speaking to. I had to tell her, but I said he had come to let her ken that the minister was taking shelter frae the rain in a farmhouse. Ay, I said he was to bide there till the flood gaed down, and that's how she has been easy a' day. I acted for the best, but I'm sair punished now; for when she heard Tammas at the door twa or three minutes syne, she ordered me to let him in, so that she could thank him for bringing the news last nicht, despite the rain. They're in the parlour. Oh, dominie, gang in and stop his mouth."

This was hard. I dared not go to the parlour. Margaret might have died at sight of me. I turned my face from Jean.

"Jean," said someone, opening the inner kitchen door, "why did you —— ?"

She stopped, and that was what turned me round. As she spoke I thought it was the young lady; when I looked I saw it was Babbie, though no longer in a gypsy's dress. Then I knew that the young lady and Babbie were one.

CHAPTER XXXIX

HOW BABBIE SPENT THE NIGHT OF AUGUST FOURTH

How had the Egyptian been spirited here from the Spittal? I did not ask the question. To interest myself in Babbie at that dire hour of Margaret's life would have been as impossible to me as to sit down to a book. To others, however, it is only an old woman on whom the parlour door of the manse has closed, only a garrulous dominie that is in pain outside it. Your eyes are on the young wife.

When Babbie was plucked off the hill, she thought as little as Gavin that her captor was Rob Dow. Close as he was to her, he was but a shadow until she screamed the second time, when he pressed her to the ground and tied his neckerchief over her mouth. Then, in the moment that power of utterance was taken from her, she saw the face that had startled her at Nanny's window. Half-carried, she was borne forward rapidly, until someone seemed to rise out of the broom and strike them both. They had only run against the doctor's trap; and huddling her into it, Dow jumped up beside her.

442

THE NIGHT OF AUGUST FOURTH

He tied her hands together with a cord. For a
time the horse feared the darkness in front more
than the lash behind; but when the rains became
terrific, it rushed ahead wildly — probably with its
eyes shut.

In three minutes Babbie went through all the
degrees of fear. In the first she thought Lord Rintoul had kidnapped her; but no sooner had her
captor resolved himself into Dow, drunk with the
events of the day and night, than in the earl's hands
would have lain safety. Next, Dow was forgotten
in the dread of a sudden death which he must
share. And lastly, the rain seemed to be driving
all other horrors back, that it might have her for
its own. Her perils increased to the unbearable as
quickly as an iron in the fire passes through the
various stages between warmth and white heat.
Then she had to do something; and as she could
not cry out, she flung herself from the dog-cart.
She fell heavily in Caddam Wood, but the rain
would not let her lie there stunned. It beat her
back to consciousness, and she sat up on her knees
and listened breathlessly, staring in the direction
the trap had taken, as if her eyes could help her
ears.

All night, I have said, the rain poured, but those
charges only rode down the deluge at intervals, as
now and again one wave greater than the others
stalks over the sea. In the first lull it appeared to

443

Babbie that the storm had swept by, leaving her to Dow. Now she heard the rubbing of the branches, and felt the torn leaves falling on her gown. She rose to feel her way out of the wood with her bound hands, then sank in terror, for someone had called her name. Next moment she was up again, for the voice was Gavin's, who was hurrying after her, as he thought, down Windy-ghoul. He was no farther away than a whisper might have carried on a still night, but she dared not pursue him, for already Dow was coming back. She could not see him, but she heard the horse whinny and the rocking of the dog-cart. Dow was now at the brute's head, and probably it tried to bite him, for he struck it, crying —

"Would you? Stand still till I find her. I heard her move this minute."

Babbie crouched upon a big stone, and sat motionless while he groped for her. Her breathing might have been tied now, as well as her mouth. She heard him feeling for her, first with his feet and then with his hands, and swearing when his head struck against a tree.

"I ken you're within hearing," he muttered, "and I'll hae you yet. I have a gully-knife in my hand. Listen!"

He severed a whin stalk with the knife, and Babbie seemed to see the gleam of the blade.

"What do I mean by wanting to kill you?" he

said, as if she had asked the question. "Do you no ken wha said to me, 'Kill this woman'? It was the Lord. 'I winna kill her,' I said, 'but I'll cart her out o' the country.' 'Kill her,' says He; 'why encumbereth she the ground?'"

He resumed his search, but with new tactics. "I see you now," he would cry, and rush forward, perhaps within a yard of her. Then she must have screamed had she had the power. When he tied that neckerchief round her mouth he prolonged her life.

Then came the second hurricane of rain, so appalling that had Babbie's hands been free she would have pressed them to her ears. For a full minute she forgot Dow's presence. A living thing touched her face. The horse had found her. She recoiled from it, but its frightened head pressed heavily on her shoulder. She rose and tried to steal away, but the brute followed, and as the rain suddenly exhausted itself she heard the dragging of the dog-cart. She had to halt.

Again she heard Dow's voice. Perhaps he had been speaking throughout the roar of the rain. If so, it must have made him deaf to his own words. He groped for the horse's head, and presently his hand touched Babbie's dress, then jumped from it, so suddenly had he found her. No sound escaped him, and she was beginning to think it possible that he had mistaken her for a bush, when his hand went over her face. He was making sure of his discovery.

"The Lord has delivered you into my hands," he said in a low voice, with some awe in it. Then he pulled her to the ground, and, sitting down beside her, rocked himself backwards and forwards, his hands round his knees. She would have bartered the world for power to speak to him.

"He wouldna hear o' my just carting you to some other countryside," he said confidentially. "'The devil would just blaw her back again,' says He, 'therefore kill her.' 'And if I kill her,' I says, 'they'll hang me.' 'You can hang yoursel',' says He. 'What wi'?' I speirs. 'Wi' the reins o' the dog-cart,' says He. 'They would break,' says I. 'Weel, weel,' says He, 'though they do hang you, nobody'll miss you.' 'That's true,' says I, 'and You are a just God.'"

He stood up and confronted her.

"Prisoner at the bar," he said, "hae ye onything to say why sentence of death shouldna be pronounced against you? She doesna answer. She kens death is her deserts."

By this time he had forgotten probably why his victim was dumb.

"Prisoner at the bar, hand back to me the soul o' Gavin Dishart. You winna? Did the devil, your master, summon you to him and say, 'Either that noble man or me maun leave Thrums?' He

did. And did you, or did you no, drag that minister, when under your spell, to the hill, and there
marry him ower the tongs? You did. Witnesses, Rob Dow and Tammas Whamond."

She was moving from him on her knees, meaning when out of arm's reach to make a dash for
life.

" Sit down," he grumbled, " or how can you expect a fair trial? Prisoner at the bar, you have
been found guilty of witchcraft."

For the first time his voice faltered.

" That's the difficulty, for witches canna die, except by burning or drowning. There's no blood
in you for my knife, and your neck wouldna twist.
Your master has brocht the rain to put out a' the
fires, and we'll hae to wait till it runs into a pool
deep enough to drown you.

" I wonder at You, God. Do You believe her
master'll mak' the pool for her? He'll rather stop
his rain. Mr. Dishart said You was mair powerful than the devil, but it doesna look like it. If
You had the power, how did You no stop this woman working her will on the minister? You kent
what she was doing, for You ken a' things. Mr.
Dishart says You ken a' things. If You do, the
mair shame to You. Would a shepherd, that could
help it, let dogs worry his sheep? Kill her! It's
fine to cry 'Kill her,' but whaur's the bonfire,
whaur's the pool? You that made the heaven and

447

the earth and all that in them is, can You no set fire to some wet whins, or change this stane into a mill-dam?"

He struck the stone with his fist, and then gave a cry of exultation. He raised the great slab in his arms and flung it from him. In that moment Babbie might have run away, but she fainted. Almost simultaneously with Dow she knew this was the stone which covered the Caddam well. When she came to, Dow was speaking, and his voice had become solemn.

"You said your master was mair powerful than mine, and I said it too, and all the time you was sitting here wi' the very pool aneath you that I have been praying for. Listen!"

He dropped a stone into the well, and she heard it strike the water.

"What are you shaking at?" he said in reproof. "Was it no yoursel' that chose the spot? Lassie, say your prayers. Are you saying them?"

He put his hand over her face, to feel if her lips were moving, and tore off the neckerchief.

And then again the rain came between them. In that rain one could not think. Babbie did not know that she had bitten through the string that tied her hands. She planned no escape. But she flung herself at the place where Dow had been standing. He was no longer there, and she fell heavily, and was on her feet again in an instant and running recklessly. Trees intercepted her, and she thought they were Dow, and wrestled with them. By-and-by she fell into Windyghoul, and there she crouched until all her senses were restored to her, when she remembered that she had been married lately.

How long Dow was in discovering that she had escaped, and whether he searched for her, no one knows. After a time he jumped into the dog-cart again, and drove aimlessly through the rain. That wild journey probably lasted two hours, and came to an abrupt end only when a tree fell upon the trap. The horse galloped off, but one of Dow's legs was beneath the tree, and there he had to lie helpless; for though the leg was little injured, he could not extricate himself. A night and day passed, and he believed that he must die; but even in this plight he did not forget the man he loved. He found a piece of slate, and in the darkness cut these words on it with his knife:—

"Me being about to die, I solemnly swear I didna see the minister marrying an Egyptian on the hill this nicht. May I burn in Hell if this is no true.   (Signed)   "Rob Dow."

This document he put in his pocket, and so preserved proof of what he was perjuring himself to deny.

CHAPTER XL

BABBIE AND MARGARET—DEFENCE OF THE MANSE
CONTINUED

The Egyptian was mournful in Windyghoul, up
which she had once danced and sung; but you
must not think that she still feared Dow. I felt
McKenzie's clutch on my arm for hours after he
left me, but she was far braver than I; indeed,
dangers at which I should have shut my eyes only
made hers gleam, and I suppose it was sheer love
of them that first made her play the coquette with
Gavin. If she cried now, it was not for herself;
it was because she thought she had destroyed him.
Could I have gone to her then, and said that Gavin
wanted to blot out the gypsy wedding, that throb-
bing little breast would have frozen at once, and
the drooping head would have been proud again,
and she would have gone away for ever without
another tear.

What do I say? I am doing a wrong to the
love these two bore each other. Babbie would not
have taken so base a message from my lips. He
would have had to say the words to her himself

450

before she believed them his. What would he want her to do now? was the only question she asked herself. To follow him was useless, for in that rain and darkness two people might have searched for each other all night in a single field. That he would go to the Spittal, thinking her in Rintoul's dog-cart, she did not doubt; and his distress was painful to her to think of. But not knowing that the burns were in flood, she under-estimated his danger.

Remembering that the mud house was near, she groped her way to it, meaning to pass the night there; but at the gate she turned away hastily, hearing from the door the voice of a man she did not know to be Nanny's brother. She wandered recklessly a short distance, until the rain began to threaten again, and then, falling on her knees in the broom, she prayed to God for guidance. When she rose, she set off for the manse.

The rain that followed the flash of lightning had brought Margaret to the kitchen.

"Jean, did you ever hear such a rain? It is trying to break into the manse."

"I canna hear you, ma'am; is it the rain you're feared at?"

"What else could it be?"

Jean did not answer.

"I hope the minister won't leave the church, Jean, till this is over?"

"Nobody would daur, ma'am. The rain'll turn the key on them all."

Jean forced out these words with difficulty, for she knew that the church had been empty, and the door locked for over an hour.

"This rain has come as if in answer to the minister's prayer, Jean."

"It wasna rain like this they wanted."

"Jean, you would not attempt to guide the Lord's hand. The minister will have to reprove the people for thinking too much of him again, for they will say that he induced God to send the rain. To-night's meeting will be remembered long in Thrums."

Jean shuddered, and said, "It's mair like an ordinary rain now, ma'am."

"But it has put out your fire, and I wanted another heater. Perhaps the one I have is hot enough, though."

Margaret returned to the parlour, and from the kitchen Jean could hear the heater tilted backward and forward in the box-iron — a pleasant, homely sound when there is happiness in the house. Soon she heard a step outside, however, and it was followed by a rough shaking of the barred door.

"Is it you, Mr. Dishart?" Jean asked nervously.

"It's me, Tammas Whamond," the precentor answered. "Unbar the door."

" What do you want ? Speak low."

" I winna speak low. Let me in. I have news for the minister's mother."

" What news ? " demanded Jean.

" Jean Proctor, as chief elder of the kirk I order you to let me do my duty."

" Whaur's the minister ? "

" He's a minister no longer. He's married a gypsy woman and run awa wi' her."

" You lie, Tammas Whamond. I believe——"

" Your belief's of no consequence. Open the door, and let me in to tell your mistress what I hae seen."

" She'll hear it first frae his ain lips if she hears it ava. I winna open the door."

" Then I'll burst it open."

Whamond flung himself at the door, and Jean, her fingers rigid with fear, stood waiting for its fall. But the rain came to her rescue by lashing the precentor until even he was forced to run from it.

" I'll be back again," he cried. " Woe to you, Jean Proctor, that hae denied your God this nicht."

" Who was that speaking to you, Jean ? " asked Margaret, re-entering the kitchen. Until the rain abated, Jean did not attempt to answer.

" I thought it was the precentor's voice," Margaret said.

Jean was a poor hand at lying, and she stuttered in her answer.

"There is nothing wrong, is there?" cried Margaret, in sudden fright. "My son —— "

"Nothing, nothing."

The words jumped from Jean to save Margaret from falling. Now she could not take them back. "I winna believe it o' him," said Jean to herself. "Let them say what they will, I'll be true to him; and when he comes back he'll find her as he left her."

"It was Lang Tammas," she answered his mistress; "but he just came to say that —— "

"Quick, Jean! what?"

"—— Mr. Dishart has been called to a sick-bed in the country, ma'am — to the farm o' Look-About-You; and as it's sic a rain, he's to bide there a' nicht."

"And Whamond came through that rain to tell me this? How good of him. Was there any other message?"

"Just that the minister hoped you would go straight to your bed, ma'am," said Jean, thinking to herself, "There can be no great sin in giving her one mair happy nicht; it may be her last."

The two women talked for a short time, and then read verse about in the parlour from the third chapter of Mark.

"This is the first night we have been left alone in the manse," Margaret said, as she was retiring to her bedroom, "and we must not grudge the minister to those who have sore need of him. I notice that you have barred the doors."

" Ay, they're barred. Nobody can win in the nicht."

"Nobody will want in, Jean," Margaret said, smiling.

" I dinna ken about that," answered Jean below her breath. " Ay, ma'am, may you sleep for baith o' us this nicht, for I daurna gang to my bed."

Jean was both right and wrong, for two persons wanted in within the next half-hour, and she opened the door to both of them. The first to come was Babbie.

So long as women sit up of nights listening for a footstep, will they flatten their faces at the window, though all without be black. Jean had not been back in the kitchen for two minutes before she raised the blind. Her eyes were close to the glass, when she saw another face almost meet hers, as you may touch your reflection in a mirror. But this face was not her own. It was white and sad. Jean suppressed a cry, and let the blind fall, as if shutting the lid on some uncanny thing.

" Won't you let me in ? " said a voice that might have been only the sob of a rain-beaten wind; " I am nearly drowned."

Jean stood like death; but her suppliant would not pass on.

" You are not afraid ? " the voice continued;

"raise the blind again, and you will see that no one need fear me."

At this request Jean's hands sought each other's company behind her back.

"Wha are you?" she asked, without stirring. "Are you — the woman?"

"Yes."

"Whaur's the minister?"

The rain again became wild, but this time it only tore by the manse as if to a conflict beyond.

"Are you aye there? I daurna let you in till I'm sure the mistress is bedded. Gang round to the front, and see if there's ony licht burning in the high west window."

"There was a light," the voice said presently, "but it was turned out as I looked."

"Then I'll let you in, and God kens I mean no wrang by it."

Babbie entered shivering, and Jean re-barred the door. Then she looked long at the woman whom her master loved. Babbie was on her knees at the hearth, holding out her hands to the dead fire.

"What a pity it's a fause face."

"Do I look so false?"

"Is it true? You're no married to him?"

"Yes, it is true."

"And yet you look as if you was fond o' him. If you cared for him, how could you do it?"

"That was why I did it."

"And him could hae had wha he liked."

"I gave up Lord Rintoul for him."

"What? Na, na; you're the Egyptian."

"You judge me by my dress."

"And soaking it is. How you're shivering — what neat fingers — what bonny little feet. I could near believe what you tell me. Aff wi' these rags, and I'll gie you on my black frock, if — if you promise me no to gang awa wi't."

So Babbie put on some clothes of Jean's, including the black frock, and stockings and shoes.

"Mr. Dishart cannot be back, Jean," she said, "before morning, and I don't want his mother to see me till he comes."

"I wouldna let you near her the nicht, though you gaed on your knees to me. But whaur is he?"

Babbie explained why Gavin had set off for the Spittal; but Jean shook her head incredulously, saying, "I canna believe you're that grand leddy, and yet ilka time I look at you I could near believe it."

In another minute Jean had something else to think of, for there came a loud rap upon the front door.

"It's Tammas Whamond back again," she moaned; "and if the mistress hears, she'll tell me to let him in."

"You shall open to me," cried a hoarse voice.

"That's no Tammas's word," Jean said in bewilderment.

"It is Lord Rintoul," Babbie whispered.

"What? Then it's truth you told me."

The knocking continued; a door upstairs opened, and Margaret spoke over the banisters.

"Have you gone to bed, Jean? Someone is knocking at the door, and a minute ago I thought I heard a carriage stop close by. Perhaps the farmer has driven Mr. Dishart home."

"I'm putting on my things, ma'am," Jean answered; then whispered to Babbie, "What's to be done?"

"He won't go away," Babbie answered. "You will have to let him into the parlour, Jean. Can she see the door from up there?"

"No; but though he was in the parlour?"

"I shall go to him there."

"Make haste, Jean," Margaret called. "If it is any persons wanting shelter, we must give it them on such a night."

"A minute, ma'am," Jean answered. To Babbie she whispered, "What shall I say to her?"

"I — I don't know," answered Babbie ruefully. "Think of something, Jean. But open the door now. Stop, let me into the parlour first."

The two women stole into the parlour.

"Tell me what will be the result o' his coming here," entreated Jean.

BABBIE AND MARGARET

" The result," Babbie said firmly, " will be that he shall go away and leave me here."

Margaret heard Jean open the front door and speak to some person or persons whom she showed into the parlour.

CHAPTER XLI

" You dare to look me in the face ! "

They were Rintoul's words. Yet Babbie had
only ventured to look up because he was so long
in speaking. His voice was low, but harsh, like
a wheel on which the brake is pressed sharply.

" It seems to be more than the man is capable
of," he added sourly.

" Do you think," Babbie exclaimed, taking fire,
" that he is afraid of you ? "

" So it seems; but I will drag him into the
light, wherever he is skulking."

Lord Rintoul strode to the door, and the brake
was off his tongue already.

" Go," said Babbie coldly, " and shout and stamp
through the house; you may succeed in frightening the women, who are the only persons in it."

" Where is he ? "

" He has gone to the Spittal to see you."

" He knew I was on the hill."

" He lost me in the darkness, and thought you
had run away with me in your trap."

460

"Ha! So he is off to the Spittal to ask me to give you back to him."

"To compel you," corrected Babbie.

"Pooh!" said the earl nervously, "that was but mummery on the hill."

"It was a marriage."

"With gypsies for witnesses. Their word would count for less than nothing. Babbie, I am still in time to save you."

"I don't want to be saved. The marriage had witnesses no court could discredit."

"What witnesses?"

"Mr. McKenzie and yourself."

She heard his teeth meet. When next she looked at him, there were tears in his eyes as well as in her own. It was perhaps the first time these two had ever been in close sympathy. Both were grieving for Rintoul.

"I am so sorry," Babbie began in a broken voice; then stopped, because they seemed such feeble words.

"If you are sorry," the earl answered eagerly, "it is not yet too late. McKenzie and I saw nothing. Come away with me, Babbie, if only in pity for yourself."

"Ah, but I don't pity myself."

"Because this man has blinded you."

"No, he has made me see."

"This mummery on the hill———"

" Why do you call it so? I believe God approved of that marriage, as He could never have countenanced yours and mine."

"God! I never heard the word on your lips before."

" I know that."

" It is his teaching, doubtless?"

" Yes."

" And he told you that to do to me as you have done was to be pleasing in God's sight?"

" No; he knows that it was so evil in God's sight that I shall suffer for it always."

" But he has done no wrong, so there is no punishment for him?"

" It is true that he has done no wrong, but his punishment will be worse, probably, than mine."

" That," said the earl, scoffing, " is not just."

" It is just. He has accepted responsibility for my sins by marrying me."

" And what form is his punishment to take?"

" For marrying me he will be driven from his church and dishonoured in all men's eyes, unless —unless God is more merciful to us than we can expect."

Her sincerity was so obvious that the earl could no longer meet it with sarcasm.

" It is you I pity now," he said, looking wonderingly at her. " Do you not see that this man has deceived you? Where was his boasted purity in meeting you by stealth, as he must have been doing, and plotting to take you from me?"

"If you knew him," Babbie answered, "you would not need to be told that he is incapable of that. He thought me an ordinary gypsy until an hour ago."

"And you had so little regard for me that you waited until the eve of what was to be our marriage, and then, laughing at my shame, ran off to marry him."

"I am not so bad as that," Babbie answered, and told him what had brought her to Thrums. "I had no thought but of returning to you, nor he of keeping me from you. We had said good-bye at the mud house door — and then we heard your voice."

"And my voice was so horrible to you that it drove you to this!"

"I — I love him so much."

What more could Babbie answer? These words told him that, if love commands, home, the friendships of a life-time, kindnesses incalculable, are at once as nought. Nothing is so cruel as love if a rival challenges it to combat.

"Why could you not love me, Babbie?" said the earl sadly. "I have done so much for you."

It was little he had done for her that was not selfish. Men are deceived curiously in such matters. When they add a new wing to their house, they do not call the action virtue; but if they give to a fellow-creature for their own gratification, they demand of God a good mark for it. Babbie, however, was in no mood to make light of the earl's gifts, and at his question she shook her head sorrowfully.

" Is it because I am too — old ? "

This was the only time he ever spoke of his age to her.

" Oh no, it is not that," she replied hastily, " I love Mr. Dishart — because he loves me, I think."

" Have I not loved you always ? "

" Never," Babbie answered simply. " If you had, perhaps then I should have loved you."

" Babbie," he exclaimed, " if ever man loved woman, and showed it by the sacrifices he made for her, I —— "

" No," Babbie said, " you don't understand what it is. Ah! I did not mean to hurt you."

" If I don't know what it is, what is it ? " he asked, almost humbly. " I scarcely know you now."

" That is it," said Babbie.

She gave him back his ring, and then he broke down pitifully. Doubtless there was good in him, but I saw him only once, and with nothing to contrast against it I may not now attempt to breathe life into the dust of his senile passion. These were the last words that passed between him and Babbie :—

" There was nothing," he said wistfully, " in this wide world that you could not have had by asking me for it. Was not that love ? "

" No," she answered. " What right have I to everything I cry for ? "

" You should never have had a care had you married me. That is love."

" It is not. I want to share my husband's cares, as I expect him to share mine."

" I would have humoured you in everything."

" You always did : as if a woman's mind were for laughing at, like a baby's passions."

" You had your passions, too, Babbie. Yet did I ever chide you for them ? That was love."

" No, it was contempt. Oh," she cried passionately, " what have not you men to answer for who talk of love to a woman when her face is all you know of her ; and her passions, her aspirations, are for kissing to sleep, her very soul a plaything ? I tell you, Lord Rintoul, and it is all the message I send back to the gentleman at the Spittal who made love to me behind your back, that this is a poor folly, and well calculated to rouse the wrath of God."

Now Jean's ear had been to the parlour keyhole for a time, but some message she had to take to Margaret, and what she risked saying was this—

" It's Lord Rintoul and a party that has been catched in the rain, and he would be obliged to you if you could gie his bride shelter for the nicht."

Thus the distracted servant thought to keep Margaret's mind at rest until Gavin came back.

" Lord Rintoul!" exclaimed Margaret. "What a pity Gavin has missed him. Of course she can stay here. Did you say I had gone to bed? I should not know what to say to a lord. But ask her to come up to me after he has gone—and, Jean, is the parlour looking tidy?"

Lord Rintoul having departed, Jean told Babbie how she had accounted to Margaret for his visit. "And she told me to gie you dry claethes and her compliments, and would you gang up to the bedroom and see her?"

Very slowly Babbie climbed the stairs. I suppose she is the only person who was ever afraid of Margaret. Her first knock on the bedroom door was so soft that Margaret, who was sitting up in bed, did not hear it. When Babbie entered the room, Margaret's first thought was that there could be no other so beautiful as this, and her second was that the stranger seemed even more timid than herself. After a few minutes' talk she laid aside her primness, a weapon she had drawn in self-defence lest this fine lady should not understand the grandeur of a manse, and at a "Call me Babbie, won't you?" she smiled.

" That is what some other person calls you!"

said Margaret archly. "Do you know that he took twenty minutes to say good-night? My dear," she added hastily, misinterpreting Babbie's silence, "I should have been sorry had he taken one second less. Every tick of the clock was a gossip, telling me how he loves you."

In the dim light a face that begged for pity was turned to Margaret.

"He does love you, Babbie?" she asked, suddenly doubtful.

Babbie turned away her face, then shook her head.

"But you love him?"

Again Babbie shook her head.

"Oh, my dear," cried Margaret, in distress, "if this is so, are you not afraid to marry him?"

She knew now that Babbie was crying, but she did not know why Babbie could not look her in the face.

"There may be times," Babbie said, most woeful that she had not married Rintoul, "when it is best to marry a man though we do not love him."

"You are wrong, Babbie," Margaret answered gravely; "if I know anything at all, it is that."

"It may be best for others."

"Do you mean for one other?" Margaret asked, and the girl bowed her head. "Ah, Babbie, you speak like a child."

"You do not understand."

467

"I do not need to be told the circumstances to know this—that if two people love each other, neither has any right to give the other up."

Babbie turned impulsively to cast herself on the mercy of Gavin's mother, but no word could she say; a hot tear fell from her eyes upon the coverlet, and then she looked at the door, as if to run away.

"But I have been too inquisitive," Margaret began; whereupon Babbie cried, "Oh no, no, no: you are very good. I have no one who cares whether I do right or wrong."

"Your parents——"

"I have had none since I was a child."

"It is the more reason why I should be your friend," Margaret said, taking the girl's hand.

"You do not know what you are saying. You cannot be my friend."

"Yes, dear, I love you already. You have a good face, Babbie, as well as a beautiful one."

Babbie could remain in the room no longer. She bade Margaret good-night and bent forward to kiss her; then drew back, like a Judas ashamed.

"Why did you not kiss me?" Margaret asked in surprise, but poor Babbie walked out of the room without answering.

Of what occurred at the manse on the following day until I reached it, I need tell little more.

RINTOUL AND BABBIE

When Babbie was tending Sam'l Farquharson's child in the Tenements, she learned of the flood in Glen Quharity, and that the greater part of the congregation had set off to the assistance of the farmers; but fearful as this made her for Gavin's safety, she kept the new anxiety from his mother. Deceived by another story of Jean's, Margaret was the one happy person in the house.

"I believe you had only a lover's quarrel with Lord Rintoul last night," she said to Babbie in the afternoon. "Ah, you see I can guess what is taking you to the window so often. You must not think him long in coming for you. I can assure you that the rain which keeps my son from me must be sufficiently severe to separate even true lovers. Take an old woman's example, Babbie. If I thought the minister's absence alarming, I should be in anguish; but as it is, my mind is so much at ease that, see, I can thread my needle."

It was in less than an hour after Margaret spoke thus tranquilly to Babbie that the precentor got into the manse.

CHAPTER XLII

MARGARET, THE PRECENTOR, AND GOD BETWEEN

UNLESS Andrew Luke, who went to Canada, be
still above ground, I am now the only survivor of
the few to whom Lang Tammas told what passed
in the manse parlour after the door closed on him
and Margaret. With the years the others lost the
details, but before I forget them the man who has
been struck by lightning will look at his arm without remembering what shrivelled it. There even
came a time when the scene seemed more vivid
to me than to the precentor, though that was only
after he began to break up.

"She was never the kind o' woman," Whamond
said, "that a body need be nane feared at. You
can see she is o' the timid sort. I couldna hae se-
lected a woman easier to speak bold out to, though
I had ha'en my pick o' them."

He was a gaunt man, sour and hard, and he
often paused in his story with a puzzled look on
his forbidding face.

"But, man, she was so michty windy o' him.
If he had wanted to put a knife into her, I believe

470

that woman would just hae telled him to take care
not to cut his hands.   Ay, and what innocent-like
she was.   If she had heard enough, afore I saw
her, to make her uneasy, I could hae begun at
once; but here she was, shaking my hand and
smiling to me, so that aye when I tried to speak
I gaed through ither.   Nobody can despise me
for it, I tell you, mair than I despise mysel'.

"I thocht to mysel', 'Let her hae her smile out,
Tammas Whamond; it's her hinmost.'   Syne wi'
shame at my cowardiness I tried to yoke to my
duty as chief elder o' the kirk, and I said to her,
as thrawn as I could speak, 'Dinna thank me;
I've done nothing for you.'

"'I ken it wasna for me you did it,' she said,
'but for him; but oh, Mr. Whamond, will that
make me think the less o' you?   He's my all,'
she says, wi' that smile back in her face, and a look
mixed up wi't that said as plain, 'and I need no
more.'   I thocht o' saying that some builds their
house upon the sand, but— dagont, dominie, it's
a solemn thing the pride mithers has in their laddies.   I mind aince my ain mither—what the devil
are you glowering at, Andrew Luke?   Do you
think I'm greeting?

"'You'll sit down, Mr. Whamond,' she says,
next.

"'No, I winna,' I said, angry-like.   'I didna
come here to sit.'

471

" I could see she thocht I was shy at being in the manse-parlour; ay, and I thocht she was pleased at me looking shy. Weel, she took my hat out o' my hand, and she put it on the chair at the door, whaur there's aye an auld chair in grand houses for the servant to sit on at family exercise.

" ' You're a man, Mr. Whamond,' says she, ' that the minister delights to honour, and so you'll oblige me by sitting in his own arm-chair.' "

Gavin never quite delighted to honour the precentor, of whom he was always a little afraid, and perhaps Margaret knew it. But you must not think less of her for wanting to gratify her son's chief elder. She thought, too, that he had just done her a service. I never yet knew a good woman who did not enjoy flattering men she liked.

" I saw my chance at that," Whamond went on, "and I says to her sternly, ' In worldly position,' I says, ' I'm a common man, and it's no for the like o' sic to sit in a minister's chair; but it has been God's will,' I says, ' to wrap around me the mantle o' chief elder o' the kirk, and if the minister falls awa frae grace, it becomes my duty to take his place.'

" If she had been looking at me, she maun hae grown feared at that, and syne I could hae gone on though my ilka word was a knock-down blow. But she was picking some things aff the chair to let me down on't.

" 'It's a pair o' mittens I'm working for the minister,' she says, and she handed them to me. Ay, I tried no to take them, but —— Oh, lads, it's queer to think how saft I was.

" 'He's no to ken about them till they're finished,' she says, terrible fond-like.

" The words came to my mouth, ' They'll never be finished,' and I could hae cursed myself for no saying them. I dinna ken how it was, but there was something pitiful in seeing her take up the mittens and begin working cheerily at one, and me kenning all the time that they would never be finished. I watched her fingers, and I said to mysel', ' Another stitch, and that maun be your last.' I said that to mysel' till I thocht it was the needle that said it, and I wondered at her no hearing.

" In the tail of the day I says, ' You needna bother; he'll never wear them,' and they sounded sic words o' doom that I rose up off the chair. Ay, but she took me up wrang, and she said, ' I see you have noticed how careless o' his ain comforts he is, and that in his zeal he forgets to put on his mittens, though they may be in his pocket a' the time. Ay,' says she, confident-like, ' but he winna forget these mittens, Mr. Whamond, and I'll tell you the reason; it's because they're his mother's work.'

" I stamped my foot, and she gae me an apologetic look, and she says, ' I canna help boasting about his being so fond o' me.'

"Ay, but here was me saying to mysel', 'Do your duty, Tammas Whamond; you sluggard, do your duty,' and without lifting my een frae her fingers I said sternly, 'The chances are,' I said, 'that these mittens will never be worn by the hands they are worked for.'

" 'You mean,' says she, 'that he'll gie them awa to some ill-off body, as he gies near a' thing he has? Ay, but there's one thing he never parts wi', and that's my work. There's a young lady in the manse the now,' says she, 'that offered to finish the mittens for me, but he would value them less if I let ony other body put a stitch into them.'

"I thocht to mysel', 'Tammas Whamond, the Lord has opened a door to you, and you'll be disgraced for ever if you dinna walk straucht in.' So I rose again, and I says, boldly this time, 'Whaur's that young leddy? I hae something to say to her that canna be kept waiting.'

" 'She's up the stair,' she says, surprised, 'but you canna ken her, Mr. Whamond, for she just came last nicht.'

" 'I ken mair o' her than you think,' says I; 'I ken what brocht her here, and I ken wha she thinks she is to be married to, and I've come to tell her that she'll never get him.'

" 'How no?' she said, amazed-like.

" 'Because,' said I, wi' my teeth thegither, 'he is already married.'

474

" Lads, I stood waiting to see her fall, and when she didna fall I just waited langer, thinking she was slow in taking it a' in.

" ' I see you ken wha she is,' she said, looking at me, ' and yet I canna credit your news.'

" ' They're true,' I cries.

" ' Even if they are,' says she, considering, ' it may be the best thing that could happen to baith o' them.'

" I sank back in the chair in fair bewilderment, for I didna ken at that time, as we a' ken now, that she was thinking o' the earl when I was thinking o' her son. Dominie, it looked to me as if the Lord had opened a door to me, and syne shut it in my face.

" Syne wi' me sitting there in a kind o' awe o' the woman's simpleness, she began to tell me what the minister was like when he was a bairn, and I was saying a' the time to mysel', ' You're chief elder o' the kirk, Tammas Whamond, and you maun speak out the next time she stops to draw breath.' They were terrible sma', common things she told me, sic as near a' mithers minds about their bairns, but the kind o' holy way she said them drove my words down my throat, like as if I was some infidel man trying to break out wi' blasphemy in a kirk.

" ' I'll let you see something,' says she, ' that I ken will interest you.' She brocht it out o' a drawer, and what do you think it was? As sure as death it was no more than some o' his hair when he was a litlin, and it was tied up sic carefully in paper that you would hae thocht it was some valuable thing.

"'Mr. Whamond,' she says solemnly, 'you've come thrice to the manse to keep me frae being uneasy about my son's absence, and you was the chief instrument under God in bringing him to Thrums, and I'll gie you a little o' that hair.'

"Dagont, what did I care about his hair? and yet to see her fondling it! I says to mysel', 'Mrs. Dishart,' I says to mysel', 'I was the chief instrument under God in bringing him to Thrums, and I've come here to tell you that I'm to be the chief instrument under God in driving him out o't.' Ay, but when I focht to bring out these words, my mouth snecked like a box.

"'Dinna gie me his hair,' was a' I could say, and I wouldna take it frae her; but she laid it in my hand, and — and syne what could I do? Ay, it's easy to speak about thae things now, and to wonder how I could hae so disgraced the position o' chief elder o' the kirk, but I tell you I was near greeting for the woman. Call me names, dominie; I deserve them all."

I did not call Whamond names for being reluctant to break Margaret's heart. Here is a confession I may make. Sometimes I say my prayers at night in a hurry, going on my knees indeed, but with as little reverence as I take a drink of water before jumping into bed, and for the same reason, because it is my nightly habit. I am only pattering words I have by heart to a chair then, and should be as well employed writing a comic Bible. At such times I pray for the earthly well-being of the precentor, though he has been dead for many years. He crept into my prayers the day he told me this story, and was part of them for so long that when they are only a recitation he is part of them still.

"She said to me," Whamond continued, "that the women o' the congregation would be fond to handle the hair. Could I tell her that the women was waur agin him than the men? I shivered to hear her.

"'Syne when they're a' sitting breathless listening to his preaching,' she says, 'they'll be able to picture him as a bairn, just as I often do in the kirk mysel'.'

"Andrew Luke, you're sneering at me, but I tell you if you had been there and had begun to say, 'He'll preach in our kirk no more,' I would hae struck you. And I'm chief elder o' the kirk.

"She says, 'Oh, Mr. Whamond, there's times in the kirk when he is praying and the glow on his face is hardly mortal, so that I fall a shaking, wi' a mixture o' fear and pride, me being his mother;

and sinful though I am to say it, I canna help thinking at sic times that I ken what the mother o' Jesus had in her heart when she found Him in the temple.'

"Dominie, it's sax-and-twenty years since I was made an elder o' the kirk. I mind the day as if it was yestreen. Mr. Carfrae made me walk hame wi' him, and he took me into the manse parlour, and he set me in that very chair. It was the first time I was ever in the manse. Ay, he little thocht that day in his earnestness, and I little thocht mysel' in the pride o' my lusty youth, that the time was coming when I would swear in that reverenced parlour. I say swear, dominie, for when she had finished I jumped to my feet, and I cried, ' Hell! ' and I lifted up my hat. And I was chief elder.

"She fell back frae my oath," he said, " and syne she took my sleeve and speired, ' What has come ower you, Mr. Whamond? Hae you onything on your mind? '

"' I've sin on it,' I roared at her. ' I have neglect o' duty on it. I am one o' them that cries " Lord, Lord," and yet do not the things which He commands. He has pointed out the way to me, and I hinna followed it.'

"' What is it you hinna done that you should hae done? ' she said. ' Oh, Mr. Whamond, if you want my help, it's yours.'

478

" ' Your son's a' the earth to you,' I cried, 'but my eldership's as muckle to me. Sax-and-twenty years hae I been an elder, and now I maun gie it up.'

" ' Wha says that?' she speirs.

" ' I say it,' I cried. ' I've shirked my duty. I gie up my eldership now. Tammas Whamond is na langer an elder o' the kirk;' ay, and I was chief elder.

" Dominie, I think she began to say that when the minister came hame he wouldna accept my resignation, but I paid no heed to her. You ken what was the sound that keeped my ears frae her words; it was the sound o' a machine coming yont the Tenements. You ken what was the sicht that made me glare through the window instead o' looking at her; it was the sight o' Mr. Dishart in the machine. I couldna speak, but I got my body atween her and the window, for I heard shouting, and I couldna doubt that it was the folk cursing him.

" But she heard too, she heard too, and she squeezed by me to the window. I couldna look out; I just walked saft-like to the parlour door, but afore I reached it she cried joyously —

" ' It's my son come back, and see how fond o' him they are. They are running at the side o' the machine, and the laddies are tossing their bonnets in the air.'

479

" 'God help you, woman!' I said to mysel', 'it canna be bonnets—it's stanes and divits mair likely that they're flinging at him.' Syne I creeped out o' the manse. Dominie, you mind I passed you in the kitchen, and didna say a word?"

Yes, I saw the precentor pass through the kitchen, with such a face on him as no man ever saw him wear again. Since Tammas Whamond died we have had to enlarge the Thrums cemetery twice; so it can matter not at all to him, and but little to me, what you who read think of him. All his life children ran from him. He was the dourest, the most unlovable man in Thrums. But may my right hand wither, and may my tongue be cancer-bitten, and may my mind be gone into a dry rot, before I forget what he did for me and mine that day.

CHAPTER XLIII

To this day we argue in the glen about the sound
mistaken by many of us for the firing of the Spittal cannon, some calling it thunder and others the
tearing of trees in the torrent. I think it must have
been the roll of stones into the Quharity from Silver Hill, of which a corner has been missing since
that day. Silver Hill is all stones, as if creation
had been riddled there, and in the sun the mica on
them shines like many pools of water.

At the roar, as they thought, of the cannon, the
farmers looked up from their struggle with the
flood to say, " That's Rintoul married," as clocks
pause simultaneously to strike the hour. Then
every one in the glen save Gavin and myself was
done with Rintoul. Before the hills had answered
the noise, Gavin was on his way to the Spittal.
The dog must have been ten minutes in overtak-
ing him, yet he maintained afterwards that it was
with him from the start. From this we see that
the shock he had got carried him some distance
before he knew that he had left the school-house.

481

It also gave him a new strength, that happily lasted longer than his daze of mind.

Gavin moved northward quicker than I came south, climbing over or wading through his obstacles, while I went round mine. After a time, too, the dog proved useful, for on discovering that it was going homeward it took the lead, and several times drew him to the right road to the Spittal by refusing to accompany him on the wrong road. Yet in two hours he had walked perhaps nine miles without being four miles nearer the Spittal. In that flood the glen milestones were three miles apart.

For some time he had been following the dog doubtfully, for it seemed to be going too near the river. When they struck a cart-track, however, he concluded rightly that they were nearing a bridge. His faith in his guide was again tested before they had been many minutes on this sloppy road. The dog stopped, whined, looked irresolute, and then ran to the right, disappearing into the mist in an instant. He shouted to it to come back, and was surprised to hear a whistle in reply. This was sufficient to make him dash after the dog, and in less than a minute he stopped abruptly by the side of a shepherd.

"Have you brocht it?" the man cried, almost into Gavin's ear; yet the roar of the water was so tremendous that the words came faintly, as if from a distance. "Wae is me; is it only you, Mr. Dishart?"

"Is it only you!" No one in the glen would have addressed a minister thus except in a matter of life or death, and Gavin knew it.

"He'll be ower late," the shepherd exclaimed, rubbing his hands together in distress. "I'm speaking o' Whinbusses' grieve. He has run for ropes, but he'll be ower late."

"Is there someone in danger?" asked Gavin, who stood, he knew not where, with this man, enveloped in mist.

"Is there no? Look!"

"There is nothing to be seen but mist; where are we?"

"We're on the high bank o' the Quharity. Take care, man; you was stepping ower into the roaring water. Lie down and tell me if he's there yet. Maybe I just think that I see him, for the sicht is painted on my een."

Gavin lay prone and peered at the river, but the mist came up to his eyes. He only knew that the river was below, from the sound,

"Is there a man down there?" he asked, shuddering.

"There was a minute syne; on a bit island."

"Why does he not speak?"

"He's senseless. Dinna move; the mist's clearing, and you'll see if he's there syne. The mist has

483

been lifting and falling that way ilka minute since
me and the grieve saw him."

The mist did not rise. It only shook like a
blanket, and then again remained stationary. But
in that movement Gavin had seen twice, first incredulously, and then with conviction.

" Shepherd," he said, rising, " it is Lord Rintoul."

" Ay, it's him; and you saw his feet was in the
water. They were dry when the grieve left me.
Mr. Dishart, the ground he is on is being washed
awa bit by bit. I tell you, the flood's greddy for
him and it'll hae him —— Look, did you see
him again ? "

" Is he living ? "

" We saw him move. Hst ! Was that a cry ? "

It was only the howling of the dog, which had
recognised its master and was peering over the
bank, the body quivering to jump, but the legs
restless with indecision.

" If we were down there," Gavin said, " we could
hold him secure till rescue comes. It is no great
jump."

" How far would you make it ? I saw him
again ! "

" It looked further that time."

" That's it ! Sometimes the ground he is on looks
so near that you think you could almost drop on
it, and the next time it's yards and yards awa. I've

stood ready for the spring, Mr. Dishart, a dozen times, but I aye sickened. I daurna do it. Look at the dog; just when it's starting to jump, it pulls itsel' back."

As it had heard the shepherd, the dog jumped at that instant.

" It sprang too far," Gavin said.

" It didna spring far enough."

They waited, and presently the mist thinned for a moment, as if it was being drawn out. They saw the earl, but there was no dog.

" Poor brute," said the shepherd, and looked with awe at Gavin.

" Rintoul is slipping into the water," Gavin answered. " You won't jump ? "

" No, I'm wae for him, and ——"

" Then I will," Gavin was about to say, but the shepherd continued, " And him only married twa hours syne."

That kept the words in Gavin's mouth for half a minute, and then he spoke them.

" Dinna think o't,' cried the shepherd, taking him by the coat. " The ground he is on is slippery. I've flung a dozen stanes at it, and them that hit it slithered off. Though you landed in the middle o't, you would slide into the water."

" He shook himsel' free o' me," the shepherd told afterwards, " and I saw him bending down and measuring the distance wi' his een as cool as

485

if he was calculating a drill o' tatties. Syne I saw his lips moving in prayer. It wasna spunk he needed to pray for, though. Next minute there was me, my very arms prigging wi' him to think better o't, and him standing ready to loup, his knees bent, and not a tremble in them. The mist lifted, and I—— Lads, I couldna gie a look to the earl. Mr. Dishart jumped; I hardly saw him, but I kent, I kent, for I was on the bank alane. What did I do? I flung mysel' down in a sweat, and if een could bore mist mine would hae done it. I thocht I heard the minister's death-cry, and may I be struck if I dinna believe now that it was a skirl o' my ain. After that there was no sound but the jaw o' the water; and I prayed, but no to God, to the mist to rise, and after an awful time it rose, and I saw the minister was safe; he had pulled the earl into the middle o' the bit island, and was rubbing him back to consciousness. I sweat when I think o't yet."

The Little Minister's jump is always spoken of as a brave act in the glen, but at such times I am silent. This is not because, being timid myself, I am without admiration for courage. My little maid says that three in every four of my poems are to the praise of prowess, and she has not forgotten how I carried her on my shoulder once to Tilliedrum to see a soldier who had won the Victoria Cross, and made her shake hands with him, though he was very drunk. Only last year one of my scholars declared to me that Nelson never said " England expects every man this day to do his duty," for which I thrashed the boy and sent him to the cooling stone. But was it brave of Gavin to jump ? I have heard some maintain that only misery made him so bold, and others that he jumped because it seemed a fine thing to risk his life for an enemy. But these are really charges of cowardice, and my boy was never a coward. Of the two kinds of courage, however, he did not then show the nobler. I am glad that he was ready for such an act, but he should have remembered Margaret and Babbie. As it was, he may be said to have forced them to jump with him. Not to attempt a gallant deed for which one has the impulse may be braver than the doing of it.

" Though it seemed as lang time," the shepherd says, " as I could hae run up a hill in, I dinna suppose it was many minutes afore I saw Rintoul opening and shutting his een. The next glint I had o' them they were speaking to ane another ; ay, and mair than speaking. They were quarrelling. I couldna hear their words, but there was a moment when I thocht they were to grapple. Lads, the memory o' that'll hing about my death-bed. There was twa men, edicated to the highest pitch, ane a lord and the other minister, and the flood was taking awa a mouthful o' their footing ilka minute, and the jaws o' destruction was gaping for them, and yet they were near fechting. We ken now it was about a woman. Ay, but does that make it less awful?"

No, that did not make it less awful. It was even awful that Gavin's first words when Rintoul opened his eyes and closed them hastily were " Where is she?" The earl did not answer; indeed for the moment the words had no meaning to him.

" How did I come here?" he asked feebly.

" You should know better than I. Where is my wife?"

" I remember now," Rintoul repeated several times. " Yes, I had left the Spittal to look for you — you were so long in coming. How did I find you?"

" It was I who found you," Gavin answered. " You must have been swept away by the flood."

" And you too?"

In a few words Gavin told how he came to be beside the earl.

" I suppose they will say you have saved my life," was Rintoul's commentary.

" It is not saved yet. If help does not come, we shall be dead men in an hour. What have you done with my wife?"

Rintoul ceased to listen to him, and shouted sums of money to the shepherd, who shook his head and bawled an answer that neither Gavin nor the earl heard. Across that thundering water only Gavin's voice could carry, the most powerful ever heard in a Thrums pulpit, the one voice that could be heard all over the Commonty during the time of the tent-preaching. Yet he never roared, as some preachers do of whom we say, "Ah, if they could hear the Little Minister's word!"

Gavin caught the gesticulating earl by the sleeve, and said, "Another man has gone for ropes. Now, listen to me; how dared you go through a marriage ceremony with her, knowing her already to be my wife?"

Rintoul did listen this time.

"How do you know I married her?" he asked sharply.

"I heard the cannon."

Now the earl understood, and the shadow on his face shook and lifted, and his teeth gleamed. His triumph might be short-lived, but he would enjoy it while he could.

"Well," he answered, picking the pebbles for his sling with care, "you must know that I could not have married her against her will. The frolic on the hill amused her, but she feared you might think it serious, and so pressed me to proceed with her marriage to-day, despite the flood."

This was the point at which the shepherd saw the minister raise his fist. It fell, however, without striking.

"Do you really think that I could doubt her?" Gavin said compassionately, and for the second time in twenty-four hours the earl learned that he did not know what love is.

For a full minute they had forgotten where they were. Now, again, the water seemed to break loose, so that both remembered their danger simultaneously, and looked up. The mist parted for long enough to show them that where had only been the shepherd, was now a crowd of men, with here and there a woman. Before the mist again came between, the minister had recognised many members of his congregation.

In his unsuccessful attempt to reach Whinbusses, the grieve had met the relief party from Thrums. Already the weavers had helped Waster Lunny to stave off ruin, and they were now on their way to Whinbusses, keeping together through fear of mist and water. Every few minutes Snecky Hobart rang his bell to bring in stragglers.

"Follow me," was all the panting grieve could say at first, but his agitation told half his story. They went with him patiently, only stopping once, and then excitedly, for they had come suddenly on Rob Dow. Rob was still lying a prisoner beneath the tree, and the grieve now remembered that he had fallen over this tree, and neither noticed the man under it, nor been noticed by the man. Fifty hands released poor Dow, and two men were commissioned to bring him along slowly while the others hurried to the rescue of the earl. They were amazed to learn from the shepherd that Mr. Dishart also was in danger, and after " Is there a woman wi' him ? " some cried, " He'll get off cheap wi' drowning," and " It's the judgment o' God."

The island on which the two men stood was now little bigger than the round tables common in Thrums, and its centre was some feet farther from the bank than when Gavin jumped. A woman, looking down at it, sickened, and would have toppled into the water, had not John Spens clutched her. Others were so stricken with awe that they forgot they had hands.

Peter Tosh, the elder, cast a rope many times, but it would not carry. The one end was then weighted with a heavy stone, and the other tied round the waists of two men. But the force of the river had been under-estimated. The stone fell short into the torrent, which rushed off with it so furiously that the men were flung upon their faces and trailed to the verge of the precipice. A score of persons sprang to their rescue, and the rope snapped. There was only one other rope, and its fate was not dissimilar. This time the stone fell into the water beyond the island, and immediately rushed down stream. Gavin seized the

491

rope, but it pressed against his body, and would
have pushed him off his feet, had not Tosh cut it.
The trunk of the tree that had fallen on Rob
Dow was next dragged to the bank and an en-
deavour made to form a sloping bridge of it. The
island, however, was now soft and unstable, and,
though the trunk was successfully lowered, it only
knocked lumps off the island, and finally it had
to be let go, as the weavers could not pull it back.
It splashed into the water, and was at once whirled
out of sight. Some of the party on the bank began hastily to improvise a rope of cravats and the
tags of the ropes still left, but the mass stood
helpless and hopeless.

"You may wonder that we could have stood
still, waiting to see the last o' them," Birse, the
post, has said to me in the school-house, "but,
dominie, I couldna hae moved, magre my neck.
I'm a hale man, but if this minute we was to hear
the voice o' the Almighty saying solemnly, 'Afore
the clock strikes again, Birse, the post, will fall
down dead of heart disease,' what do you think
you would do? I'll tell you. You would stand
whaur you are, and stare, tongue-tied, at me till I
dropped. How do I ken? By the teaching o'
that nicht. Ay, but there's a mair important thing
I dinna ken, and that is whether I would be pal-
sied wi' fear like the earl, or face death with the
calmness o' the minister."

Indeed, the contrast between Rintoul and Gavin was now impressive. When Tosh signed that the weavers had done their all and failed, the two men looked in each other's faces, and Gavin's face was firm and the earl's working convulsively. The people had given up attempting to communicate with Gavin save by signs, for though they heard his sonorous voice, when he pitched it at them, they saw that he caught few words of theirs. " He heard our skirls," Birse said, "but couldna grip the words ony mair than we could hear the earl. And yet we screamed, and the minister didna. I've heard o' Highlandmen wi' the same gift, so that they could be heard across a glen."

" We must prepare for death," Gavin said solemnly to the earl, " and it is for your own sake that I again ask you to tell me the truth. Worldly matters are nothing to either of us now, but I implore you not to carry a lie into your Maker's presence."

" I will not give up hope," was all Rintoul's answer, and he again tried to pierce the mist with offers of reward. After that he became doggedly silent, fixing his eyes on the ground at his feet. I have a notion that he had made up his mind to confess the truth about Babbie when the water had eaten the island as far as the point at which he was now looking.

493

CHAPTER XLIV

OUT of the mist came the voice of Gavin, clear and strong —

" If you hear me, hold up your hands as a sign."

They heard, and none wondered at his voice crossing the chasm while theirs could not. When the mist cleared, they were seen to have done as he bade them. Many hands remained up for a time because the people did not remember to bring them down, so great was the awe that had fallen on all, as if the Lord was near.

Gavin took his watch from his pocket, and he said —

" I am to fling this to you. You will give it to Mr. Ogilvy, the schoolmaster, as a token of the love I bear him."

The watch was caught by James Langlands, and handed to Peter Tosh, the chief elder present.

" To Mr. Ogilvy," Gavin continued, " you will also give the chain. You will take it off my neck when you find the body.

" To each of my elders, and to Hendry Munn,

494

kirk-officer, and to my servant Jean, I leave a book, and they will go to my study and choose it for themselves.

" I also leave a book for Nanny Webster, and I charge you, Peter Tosh, to take it to her, though she be not a member of my church.

" The pictorial Bible with ' To my son on his sixth birthday ' on it, I bequeath to Rob Dow. No, my mother will want to keep that. I give to Rob Dow my Bible with the brass clasp.

" It is my wish that every family in the congregation should have some little thing to remember me by. This you will tell my mother.

" To my successor I leave whatsoever of my papers he may think of any value to him, including all my notes on Revelation, of which I meant to make a book. I hope he will never sing the paraphrases.

" If Mr. Carfrae's health permits, you will ask him to preach the funeral sermon; but if he be too frail, then you will ask Mr. Trail, under whom I sat in Glasgow. The illustrated ' Pilgrim's Progress ' on the drawers in my bedroom belongs to Mr. Trail, and you will return it to him with my affection and compliments.

" I owe five shillings to Hendry Munn for mending my boots, and a smaller sum to Baxter, the mason. I have two pounds belonging to Rob Dow, who asked me to take charge of them for him. I owe no other man anything, and this you will bear in mind if Matthew Cargill, the flying stationer, again brings forward a claim for the price of Whiston's 'Josephus,' which I did not buy from him.

"Mr. Moncur, of Aberbrothock, had agreed to assist me at the Sacrament, and will doubtless still lend his services. Mr. Carfrae or Mr. Trail will take my place if my successor is not elected by that time. The Sacrament cups are in the vestry press, of which you will find the key beneath the clock in my parlour. The tokens are in the topmost drawer in my bedroom.

"The weekly prayer-meeting will be held as usual on Thursday at eight o'clock, and the elders will officiate.

"It is my wish that the news of my death be broken to my mother by Mr. Ogilvy, the schoolmaster, and by no other. You will say to him that this is my solemn request, and that I bid him discharge it without faltering and be of good cheer.

"But if Mr. Ogilvy be not now alive, the news of my death will be broken to my mother by my beloved wife. Last night I was married on the hill, over the tongs, but with the sanction of God, to her whom you call the Egyptian, and despite what has happened since then, of which you will soon have knowledge, I here solemnly declare that

she is my wife, and you will seek for her at the
Spittal or elsewhere till you find her, and you will
tell her to go to my mother and remain with her
always, for these are the commands of her husband."

It was then that Gavin paused, for Lord Rintoul had that to say to him which no longer could
be kept back. All the women were crying sore,
and also some men whose eyes had been dry at the
coffining of their children.

"Now I ken," said Cruickshanks, who had been
an atheist, "that it's only the fool wha' says in his
heart, 'There is no God.'"

Another said, "That's a man."

Another said, "That man has a religion to last
him all through."

A fourth said, "Behold, the Kingdom of Heaven
is at hand."

A fifth said, "That's our minister. He's the minister o' the Auld Licht Kirk o' Thrums. Woe is
me, we're to lose him."

Many cried, "Our hearts was set hard against
him. O Lord, are You angry wi' Your servants
that You're taking him frae us just when we ken
what he is?"

Gavin did not hear them, and again he spoke :—

"My brethren, God is good. I have just learned
that my wife is with my dear mother at the manse.
I leave them in your care and in His."

No more he said of Babbie, for the island was become very small.

"The Lord calls me hence. It is only for a little time I have been with you, and now I am going away, and you will know me no more. Too great has been my pride because I was your minister, but He who sent me to labour among you is slow to wrath; and He ever bore in mind that you were my first charge. My people, I must say to you, 'Farewell.'"

Then, for the first time, his voice faltered, and wanting to go on he could not. "Let us read," he said, quickly, "in the Word of God in the fourteenth of Matthew, from the twenty-eighth verse."

He repeated these four verses:—

"'And Peter answered Him and said, Lord, if it be Thou, bid me come unto Thee on the water.

"'And He said, Come. And when Peter was come down out of the ship, he walked on the water, to go to Jesus.

"'But when he saw the wind boisterous, he was afraid; and beginning to sink, he cried, saying, Lord, save me.

"'And immediately Jesus stretched forth His hand, and caught him, and said unto him, O thou of little faith, wherefore didst thou doubt?'"

After this Gavin's voice was again steady, and he said, "The sand-glass is almost run out. Dearly beloved, with what words shall I bid you good-bye?"

498

END OF THE TWENTY-FOUR HOURS

Many thought that these were to be the words, for the mist parted, and they saw the island tremble and half of it sink.

"My people," said the voice behind the mist, "this is the text I leave with you: 'Lay not up for yourselves treasures upon earth, where moth and rust doth corrupt, and where thieves break through and steal; but lay up for yourselves treasures in heaven, where neither moth nor rust doth corrupt, and where thieves do not break through nor steal.' That text I read in the flood, where the hand of God has written it. All the pound-notes in the world would not dam this torrent for a moment, so that we might pass over to you safely. Yet it is but a trickle of water, soon to be dried up. Verily, I say unto you, only a few hours ago the treasures of earth stood between you and this earl, and what are they now compared to this trickle of water? God only can turn rivers into a wilderness, and the water-springs into dry ground. Let His Word be a lamp unto your feet and a light unto your path; may He be your refuge and your strength. Amen."

This amen he said quickly, thinking death was now come. He was seen to raise his hands, but whether to Heaven, or involuntarily to protect his face as he fell, none was sure, for the mist again filled the chasm. Then came a clap of stillness. No one breathed.

THE LITTLE MINISTER

But the two men were not yet gone, and Gavin spoke once more.

"Let us sing in the twenty-third Psalm."

He himself raised the tune, and so long as they heard his voice they sang—

> "The Lord's my shepherd, I'll not want;
> He makes me down to lie
> In pastures green; He leadeth me
> The quiet waters by.
>
> "My soul He doth restore again;
> And me to walk doth make
> Within the paths of righteousness
> Ev'n for His own name's sake.
>
> "Yea, though I walk in Death's dark vale,
> Yet will I fear none ill;
> For Thou art with me; and Thy rod
> And staff——"

But some had lost the power to sing in the first verse, and others at "Death's dark vale," and when one man found himself singing alone he stopped abruptly. This was because they no longer heard the minister.

"O Lord!" Peter Tosh cried, "lift the mist, for it's mair than we can bear."

The mist rose slowly, and those who had courage to look saw Gavin praying with the earl. Many could not look, and some of them did not even see Rob Dow jump.

For it was Dow, the man with the crushed leg,

who saved Gavin's life, and flung away his own for it. Suddenly he was seen on the edge of the bank, holding one end of the improvised rope in his hand. As Tosh says —

" It all happened in the opening and shutting o' an eye. It's a queer thing to say, but though I prayed to God to take awa the mist, when He did raise it I couldna look. I shut my een tight, and held my arm afore my face, like ane feared o' being struck. Even when I daured to look, my arm was shaking so that I could see Rob both above it and below it. He was on the edge, crouching to leap. I didna see wha had haud o' the other end o' the rope. I heard the minister cry, ' No, Dow, no!' and it gaed through me as quick as a stab that if Rob jumped he would knock them both into the water. But he did jump, and you ken how it was that he didna knock them off."

It was because he had no thought of saving his own life. He jumped, not at the island, now little bigger than the seat of a chair, but at the edge of it, into the foam, and with his arm outstretched. For a second the hand holding the rope was on the dot of land. Gavin tried to seize the hand; Rintoul clutched the rope. The earl and the minister were dragged together in safety, and both left the water senseless. Gavin was never again able to lift his left hand higher than his head. Dow's body was found next day near the school-house.

CHAPTER XLV

TALK OF A LITTLE MAID SINCE GROWN TALL

MY scholars have a game they call "The Little Minister," in which the boys allow the girls as a treat to join. Some of the characters in the real drama are omitted as of no importance — the dominie, for instance — and the two best fighters insist on being Dow and Gavin. I notice that the game is finished when Dow dives from a haystack, and Gavin and the earl are dragged to the top of it by a rope. Though there should be another scene, it is only a marriage, which the girls have, therefore, to go through without the help of the boys. This warns me that I have come to an end of my story for all except my little maid. In the days when she sat on my knee and listened, it had no end, for after I told her how her father and mother were married a second time, she would say, "And then I came, didn't I? Oh, tell me about me!" So it happened that when she was no higher than my staff she knew more than I could write in another book, and many a time she solemnly told me what I had told her, as —

502

"Would you like me to tell you a story? Well, it's about a minister, and the people wanted to be bad to him, and then there was a flood, and a flood is lochs falling instead of rain, and so of course he was nearly drownded, and he preached to them till they liked him again, and so they let him marry her, and they like her awful too, and, just think! it was my father; and that's all. Now tell me about grandmother when father came home."

I told her once again that Margaret never knew how nearly Gavin was driven from his kirk. For Margaret was as one who goes to bed in the day-time and wakes in it, and is not told that there has been a black night while she slept. She had seen her son leave the manse the idol of his people, and she saw them rejoicing as they brought him back. Of what occurred at the Jaws, as the spot where Dow had saved two lives is now called, she learned, but not that these Jaws snatched him, and her, from an ignominy more terrible than death; for she never knew that the people had meditated driving him from his kirk. This Thrums is bleak and perhaps forbidding, but there is a moment of the day when a setting sun dyes it pink, and the people are like their town. Thrums was never colder in times of snow than were his congregation to their minister when the Great Rain began, but his fortitude rekindled their hearts. He was an obstinate minister, and love had led him a dance,

THE LITTLE MINISTER

but in the hour of trial he had proved himself a man.

When Gavin reached the manse, and saw not only his mother but Babbie, he would have kissed them both; but Babbie could only say, " She does not know," and then run away crying. Gavin put his arm round his mother, and drew her into the parlour, where he told her who Babbie was. Now Margaret had begun to love Babbie already, and had prayed to see Gavin happily married; but it was a long time before she went upstairs to look for his wife, and kiss her and bring her down. " Why was it a long time? " my little maid would ask, and I had to tell her to wait until she was old, and had a son, when she would find out for herself.

While Gavin and the earl were among the waters, two men were on their way to Mr. Carfrae's home, to ask him to return with them and preach the Auld Licht kirk of Thrums vacant; and he came, though now so done that he had to be wheeled about in a little coach. He came in sorrow, yet resolved to perform what was asked of him if it seemed God's will; but, instead of banishing Gavin, all he had to do was to re-marry him and kirk him, both of which things he did, sitting in his coach, as many can tell. Lang Tammas spoke no more against Gavin, but he would not go to the marriage, and he insisted on resigning his eldership for a year and a day. I think he

504

only once again spoke to Margaret. She was in
the manse garden when he was passing, and she
asked him if he would tell her now why he had
been so agitated when he visited her on the day
of the flood. He answered gruffly, "It's no business o' yours." Dr. McQueen was Gavin's best
man. He died long ago of scarlet fever. So severe
was the epidemic that for a week he was never in
bed. He attended fifty cases without suffering,
but as soon as he had bent over Hendry Munn's
youngest boys, who both had it, he said, "I'm
smitted," and went home to die. You may be
sure that Gavin proved a good friend to Micah
Dow. I have the piece of slate on which Rob
proved himself a good friend to Gavin; it was in
his pocket when we found the body. Lord Rintoul returned to his English estates, and never re-
visited the Spittal. The last thing I heard of him
was that he had been offered the Lord-Lieuten-
antship of a county, and had accepted it in a long
letter, in which he began by pointing out his unworthiness. This undid him, for the Queen, or
her councillors, thinking from his first page that
he had declined the honour, read no further, and
appointed another man. Waster Lunny is still
alive, but has gone to another farm. Sanders
Webster, in his gratitude, wanted Nanny to become
an Auld Licht, but she refused, saying, "Mr.
Dishart is worth a dozen o' Mr. Duthie, and I'm

terrible fond o' Mrs. Dishart, but Established I was born, and Established I'll remain till I'm carried out o' this house feet foremost."

"But Nanny went to Heaven for all that," my little maid told me. "Jean says people can go to Heaven though they are not Auld Lichts, but she says it takes them all their time. Would you like me to tell you a story about my mother putting glass on the manse dyke? Well, my mother and my father is very fond of each other, and once they was in the garden, and my father kissed my mother, and there was a woman watching them over the dyke, and she cried out — something naughty."

"It was Tibbie Birse," I said, "and what she cried was, 'Mercy on us, that's the third time in half an hour!' So your mother, who heard her, was annoyed, and put glass on the wall."

"But it's me that is telling you the story. You are sure you don't know it? Well, they asked father to take the glass away, and he wouldn't, but he once preached at mother for having a white feather in her bonnet, and at another time he preached at her for being too fond of him. Jean told me. That's all."

No one seeing Babbie going to church demurely on Gavin's arm could guess her history. Sometimes I wonder whether the desire to be a gypsy again ever comes over her for a mad hour, and whether, if so, Gavin takes such measures to cure her as he threatened in Caddam Wood. I suppose not; but here is another story :—

" When I ask mother to tell me about her once being a gypsy she says I am a bad 'quisitive little girl, and to put on my hat and come with her to the prayer-meeting; and when I asked father to let me see mother's gypsy frock he made me learn Psalm forty-eight by heart. But once I see'd it, and it was a long time ago, as long as a week ago. Micah Dow gave me rowans to put in my hair, and I like Micah, because he calls me Miss, and so I woke in my bed because there was noises, and I ran down to the parlour, and there was my mother in her gypsy frock, and my rowans was in her hair, and my father was kissing her, and when they saw me they jumped; and that's all.

" Would you like me to tell you another story ? It is about a little girl. Well, there was once a minister and his wife, and they hadn't no little girls, but just little boys, and God was sorry for them, so He put a little girl in a cabbage in the garden, and when they found her they were glad. Would you like me to tell you who the little girl was ? Well, it was me, and, ugh! I was awful cold in the cabbage. Do you like that story ? "

" Yes; I like it best of all the stories I know."

"So do I like it, too. Couldn't nobody help

loving me, 'cause I'm so nice? Why am I so fearful nice?"

"Because you are like your grandmother."

"It was clever of my father to know when he found me in the cabbage that my name was Margaret. Are you sorry grandmother is dead?"

"I am glad your mother and father were so good to her and made her so happy."

"Are you happy?"

"Yes."

"But when I am happy I laugh."

"I am old, you see, and you are young."

"I am nearly six. Did you love grandmother? Then why did you never come to see her? Did grandmother know you was here? Why not? Why didn't I know about you till after grandmother died?"

"I'll tell you when you are big."

"Shall I be big enough when I am six?"

"No, not till your eighteenth birthday."

"But birthdays comes so slow. Will they come quicker when I am big?"

"Much quicker."

On her sixth birthday Micah Dow drove my little maid to the school-house in the doctor's gig, and she crept beneath the table and whispered —

"Grandfather!"

"Father told me to call you that if I liked, and I like," she said when I had taken her upon my knee. "I know why you kissed me just now. It was because I looked like grandmother. Why do you kiss me when I look like her?"

"Who told you I did that?"

"Nobody didn't tell me. I just found out. I loved grandmother too. She told me all the stories she knew."

"Did she ever tell you a story about a black dog?"

"No. Did she know one?"

"Yes, she knew it."

"Perhaps she had forgotten it?"

"No, she remembered it."

"Tell it to me."

"Not till you are eighteen."

"But will you not be dead when I am eighteen? When you go to Heaven, will you see grandmother?"

"Yes."

"Will she be glad to see you?"

My little maid's eighteenth birthday has come, and I am still in Thrums, which I love, though it is beautiful to none, perhaps, save to the very done, who lean on their staves and look long at it, having nothing else to do till they die. I have lived to rejoice in the happiness of Gavin and Babbie; and if at times I have suddenly had to turn away my head after looking upon them in their home surrounded by their children, it was but a moment's envy that I could not help. Margaret never knew of the dominie in the glen. They wanted to tell her of me, but I would not have it. She has been long gone from this world; but sweet memories of her still grow, like honeysuckle, up the white walls of the manse, smiling in at the parlour window and beckoning from the door, and for some filling all the air with fragrance. It was not she who raised the barrier between her and me, but God Himself; and to those who maintain otherwise, I say they do not understand the purity of a woman's soul. During the years she was lost to me her face ever came between me and ungenerous thoughts, and now I can say, all that is carnal in me is my own, and all that is good I got from her. Only one bitterness remains. When I found Gavin in the rain, when I was fighting my way through the flood, when I saw how the hearts of the people were turned against him — above all, when I found Whamond in the manse — I cried to God, making promises to Him, if He would spare the lad for Margaret's sake, and He spared him; but these promises I have not kept.

THE END.

Why did Barrie write of a gypsy?
Her freedom from convention enabled her to do the good she did.
He wrote of two love affairs that had obstacles.